Michael Hardcastle was born in Leeds in Yorkshire. After leaving school he served in the Royal Army Educational Corps before embarking on a career in journalism, working in a number of roles for provincial daily newspapers from reporter to chief feature writer.

He has written more than one hundred and forty children's books since his first was published in 1966, but still finds time to visit schools and colleges all over Britain to talk about books and writing. In 1988 he was awarded an MBE in recognition of his services to children's books. He is married and lives in Beverley, Yorkshire.

The Striker's Revenge

Michael Hardcastle

Goal Kings
BOOK FIVE

faber and faber

First published in 2001
by Faber and Faber Limited
3 Queen Square London WC1N 3AU
Published in the United States by Faber and Faber Inc.
a division of Farrar, Straus and Giroux Inc., New York

Typeset by Avon Dataset, Bidford-on-Avon, Warwickshire
Printed and bound in England by Mackays of Chatham PLC,
Chatham, Kent

A CIP record for this book
is available from the British Library

ISBN   0–571–20554–2

2 4 6 8 10 9 7 5 3 1

Contents

1 *Rewarding the Winners*

Just as they were turning into the passage-way beside The Village Bistro Josh Rowley grabbed his team-mate by the elbow. 'Listen, Dom, something I've got to ask you,' he said in a soft, urgent voice. 'You'll tell me the truth, won't you?'

Dominic Allenby turned. 'Depends what it is,' he replied coolly. 'It's not just some girl you're fancying, is it? I mean, that's all the rest of the guys seem to be thinking about at the moment. Danny said that Andrea –'

'No, no, nothing like that,' Josh cut in hurriedly. 'I've got enough trouble just having a sister. Chrissie can be a real pain when she's in the mood. No, it's about the Player-of-the-Season Award. I know we'll all hear who it is in the next hour or two but, well, I just thought you might have some inside information. With your mum being the coach and making all the decisions . . .'

His voice trailed away as he saw Dominic's frown deepening. 'Josher, you know the score. It's never altered since Mum took over. She tells me nothing and I tell her nothing about us, the team. You all know I've never spied on anyone. Well, it works the other way, too – has to. So you're wasting your time even thinking I may know something. When she tells us who's been chosen it will be just as big a surprise to me.'

'OK, OK, I accept that,' his tall, fair-haired team-mate acknowledged. 'But you must have thought about it, worked out who you think *deserves* it. Personally, I'd give it to Danny. Not just because he's skipper, though that counts a lot because he's also so enthusiastic, isn't he, a real leader. Your mum said that once. And also there aren't many better goalkeepers in the whole Highlea Sunday League, are there? I think he's a certainty when Sam Saxton picks his team for the county match.'

'You're only saying that because Danny is a defender, like you. Defenders' Union sticking up for each other, as usual,' Dominic pointed out with a grin.

'No I'm not!' Josh protested. 'Anyway, I'm not really a defender. I scored loads of goals the season before last when I was playing in my proper position as striker. *And* I also got five goals last season when I went up for corners and free kicks. The coach says I'm always likely to score then because I can outjump anyone in the box. Oh, and you shouldn't start knocking defenders. You're one yourself.'

'True, though I used to be a striker once. Actually, I quite like playing at the back. In some ways, it's easier facing the ball all the time. The coach thinks I had my best season after a bit of a shaky start.'

'So maybe she'll give *you* the Player-of-the-Season Award! I mean, we all agree your mum is the fairest coach we've ever had. Treats everybody the same. Well, more or less. None of us would really object if you got it, Dom. So, how about it?'

The stocky central defender ran his fingers through his russet hair and then shook his head. 'No chance. She'd see that as favouritism even if no one else did. I'd only be embarrassed if she did. Anyway, I've had that award in the past, so I'm not desperate for it.'

'So who do you think will get it tonight?' Josh persisted. Once he'd got his teeth into a subject he didn't like to let go. Moreover, he hadn't given up hope that he himself might be the winner. After all, Dominic's mum had told him several times that he'd made 'a big contribution' to the Goal Kings' triumph in winning the Championship in the season that ended only three months earlier.

'Oh, probably Reuben or Davey. They're strikers, aren't they, so they're usually the ones that get the glamour treatment.' Dominic thought he'd said enough but suddenly remembered someone else. 'Oh, I suppose Kieren's in with a chance. I'm sure *he* thinks so, from what Mum said the other day.'

Josh was on to that revelation in a flash. 'You said your mum didn't discuss team things with you! So how come you were talking about Kieren Kelly's prospects?'

'Josher, we weren't discussing KK's prospects, as you put it,' Dominic replied with a deep sigh. 'All that happened was that Jakki Kelly rang Mum the other day. I knew it was her because I answered the phone. And it was just a friendly chat. But Mrs K mentioned that Kieren felt he was a certainty for the trial match. *Therefore* he probably also feels he's got a good chance of picking up our Award. Remember, he did play pretty well most of last season, better than I've ever seen him.'

'But KK's a defender ...' Josh was beginning to say when Dominic said sharply: 'Look, it's time we got inside. Oh, and here's Davey himself. Why don't you ask him who he fancies? If he's honest he'll probably pick himself or his mate Reuben.'

Josh, however, decided there was nothing to be gained by interrogating the team-mate who, physically, was such a contrast to himself and who had the role Josh coveted: centre-forward. Instead, he just raised his eyebrows and said, 'Hi, Davey.'

'The pair of you look like conspirators,' Davey grinned by way of greeting. 'What are you up to, then?'

'Oh, nothing,' Josh replied as innocently as possible. 'Just chatting about the new season. Can't believe we don't play our first game for another two weeks. We're dead keen to get started, aren't we, Dom?'

'Thought you might have been talking about who's going to get the Player-of-the-Season Award,' Davey remarked. 'I saw Danny the other day in that sports shop in Scorton and he reckons Reuben is a certainty. I agree with him. Lefty really did have a fantastic season after Mrs Allenby told him to get forward more often and score some goals for us.'

'Yeah, you could be right, Davey,' Josh murmured while Dominic simply nodded his agreement. Then, without another word, all three turned and headed for the room at the rear of the Bistro that had been booked by Jane Allenby for Rodale Goal Kings' Presentation Evening.

To their delight they found that it had been decked out in the team's purple-and-white colours and a large banner proclaiming 'Champions! Champions!' was suspended above a table bearing the Sunday League trophy as its centrepiece. Alongside it were clusters of statuettes and boxed medals.

Jane Allenby was talking cheerfully to a parent at that moment, while standing beside her was the owner of The Village Bistro,

Taylor Hill, beaming as if he himself were about to receive an award. He actually had his hand on his son's shoulder in the manner of someone posing for the kind of family photo that was popular at least a hundred years earlier.

It was a scene that immediately amused Dominic. 'Hey,' he whispered to Josh, 'there's another candidate for you. Maybe Larry Hill's going to get the award because his dad's let us have this meeting room at a special price, or even for free!'

'Never!' exclaimed Josh, though he wasn't completely sure Dominic was joking. In his view Larry was lucky to be playing for the Goal Kings. He had managed a few goals as Davey's co-striker but his general clumsiness caused him to miss many glaring openings to the despair of his team-mates. His dad, of course, had the idea that Larry would be an international one day. It had occurred to Josh more than once that if Larry were missing from the side then he himself would be the best player available to replace him as an out-and-out striker.

The room was filling up rapidly and Danny

Loxham, for one, was pleased to see that some food had been provided in dishes lined up on tables placed against a blank wall. As the Kings' skipper he felt he owed it to the coach and his team-mates to be supremely fit at all times. Already today he'd had a work-out in a gym where he went for boxing training and had also played some very vigorous badminton at the leisure centre.

'I'm starving – wish we could start on those sausage rolls right away,' he murmured to Reuben Jones. 'How about you, Lefty?'

But Reuben, famed for his left-foot skills as well as for the colour of his hair, which was so fair it was almost white, just shrugged. 'Not bothered, really. Mum was out at the dentist's all afternoon so I had to get all the rest of the kids' teas on my own. Put me right off eating, that did!'

Reuben had the largest collection of brothers and sisters that any of the Kings had heard of and his team-mates sympathized with his family duties, made all the more onerous because he was the eldest.

Now someone was tapping loudly with a knife handle on a table top before calling for silence. Conversations died away and everyone turned towards the speaker, Taylor Hill, who seemed to have assumed the role of host for the evening, despite the fact that he wasn't even on the committee of the Friends of the Goal Kings, the organization which helped raise money for the squad.

'Ladies and gentlemen and, of course, the most important persons here tonight, the Goal Kings themselves!' he boomed. 'If I may have your attention. Thank you *so* much. Well, it's my great pleasure to introduce you to someone who needs absolutely no introduction at all, our Championship-winning coach, Jane Allenby.'

Not everyone was sure whether to clap at that point, so some did and some didn't and the applause was rather scattered. Jane, however, quickly held up a hand, smiled a little nervously and then said quietly: 'I don't think you should be applauding me. We're here tonight to celebrate what the *team* did. They're the ones who deserve the cheers. They're the ones who won the Sunday League Championship in such a marvellous way, with practically the last kick of the very last game of the season. As you'll remember – well, most of us will never forget – Davey's winning goal came from the penalty spot. What terrific nerve it took to convert that penalty when to miss it would have meant, almost certainly, that our chance of the title was gone. It was a wonderful, wonderful moment for all of us, thanks to Davey.'

She paused for breath and several people took the hint. This time the clapping was loud and energetic and accompanied by cheering. Davey, who'd experienced an avalanche of congratulations when scoring his clinching goal, still turned a little pink as friends and supporters grinned at him and held thumbs aloft. He received a fond smile from his mum and a wide grin from his sister Katie, who'd recently decided that she quite liked football. Because she was a remarkably pretty girl she attracted glances from several of the boys.

'Told you,' Dominic muttered to Josh, who'd remained by his side. 'Davey will get the award.'

Josh nodded but didn't say anything. His own hopes hadn't completely vanished but he started to wonder if there might be some other reward for him besides the customary Championship medal. Then his attention was caught by the arrival of Sam Saxton, who had been Josh's first coach when he joined the Goal Kings and who now had a role selecting schoolboy teams for the county. Was Sam here to announce who he was picking from the Goal Kings? If so, then Josh might hear some good news after all.

'I don't intend to make a long speech – you don't want that – but I just want to say how proud I am of the way the boys conducted themselves throughout the season,' Jane had resumed. 'I had hardly a moment's trouble with any of them. Well, none that I'd mention in public!' That provoked some laughter and Jane, looking a little more at ease now, smiled her appreciation.

'I think I've been extraordinarily lucky because I've been the coach for little more than a season. I've been extra lucky because of the quality of the players I've got. The Goal Kings possess some exceptional talent and that's why we *are* the champions. All teams have to be ambitious and our ambition now is to remain champions. Someone once said that it's harder to hold on to a title than to win it in the first place. Well, I'm determined to prove that's false thinking. I'm sure the boys feel exactly the same.'

More applause broke out to greet that statement and one or two people shouted the slogan that the team had made their own: Kings Rule!

She waited for the noise to subside and then added: 'Well, I'm not going to say any more about the future, except to mention that I hope you will all be there to cheer us on at our first home match against Torridon in a fortnight's time. Obviously we'll want to start the new season on a winning note. Right then, let's get on with the main purpose of the evening, presenting the winners with their medals and trophies. We don't want the suspense to go on too long, do we, otherwise you won't be able to enjoy the good things that Taylor Hill has so generously provided for everyone.'

Jane glanced at the man still standing beside her and the Bistro owner beamed like a lighthouse. Larry managed to edge away nearer to where Danny was standing. His skipper, he noticed, had already raided the good things and was furtively slipping spicy crisps into his mouth when he felt no one was looking.

'Right,' she concluded, 'we've been looking back to the past season. But it seems only fair to look back just a little further and remember someone who made a huge contribution to the present success of the Goal Kings, to a predecessor of mine, Sam Saxton. He has never lost his interest in the team. Sam has kindly agreed to present the prizes. Most of you will know that Sam has another football role now. So we hope he'll continue to attend our matches. Sam.'

Taylor Hill's smile faded as he had to step back to allow the former coach to stand beside the table. While Jane read out the details of the awards Sam shook hands with each recipient and handed over the gleaming silver Championship trophy and then a medal to each of the sixteen-strong squad. There should have been a seventeenth player but Marc (Foggy) Thrale wasn't present. Jane had wondered whether he'd turn up but decided on balance he probably wouldn't. After all, Foggy, a combative midfielder renowned for the strength of his voice as well as for his high opinion of himself, had walked out on the Kings towards the end of the season.

Danny, after hastily brushing crumbs from his lips, raised the trophy above his head to tumultuous applause. He had to hold it up so long for the benefit of photographers that even his strong arms began to ache. He wished newspaper cameramen had been present but Jane had told him she'd arranged for the press to turn up in good time to take a team photograph before the Torridon match.

'And now for the individual honours,' Jane announced. 'Personally, I'd like to give the Player-of-the-Season Award to every single member of the squad. Naturally, that's impossible. I found the job of choosing just one boy practically impossible, too. In the end, I settled on the one who scored so many vital goals for us, none more vital than that penalty against those old rivals of ours, Clocklane Strikers. You all know who that is – Davey Stroud!'

Everyone turned to look at him. All Davey could think about at that moment was how glad he was that Mrs Allenby hadn't mentioned his size. Almost always when a coach or a teacher learned that he was a striker the response was on the lines of 'Oh, aren't you rather on the small side for that role?' Well, he'd proved this past season that size didn't matter at all when it came to scoring goals. In any case, he could jump higher than most of his team-mates when he needed to; and he possessed electric pace. Davey had no doubt at all that he thoroughly deserved his award. He took it with both hands and swung round to display the shining statuette high above his head, just as Danny had done with the League trophy. Once again, the cheers rang out.

'Well done, Davo,' said Danny, coming up to slap him on the back, so covering up his own disappointment. The Kings' skipper really had believed that the honour was coming to him because he felt he'd been an outstanding success. What's more, Jane had told him umpteen times how much she valued his leadership as well as his flying saves.

'And finally, there's a special award for the player who, in my opinion, showed the most improvement over the season. In his case, he could also be regarded as the Kings' star newcomer, Reuben Jones. Come on, Reuben, you thoroughly deserve this trophy.'

Reuben raised his eyebrows but that was just about his only sign of emotion as he took his reward, a slightly smaller version of Davey's. He, too, had been conjecturing about his own chance of collecting the main award, not least because he'd scored a hatful of goals himself, besides setting up many of Davey's. It was Jane who'd recruited him from his previous team, Stonecreek Pirates, and then persuaded him to try his luck up front more often. As he thanked her he couldn't help noting that he didn't receive the hug that Davey got from her. That rather confirmed Reuben's impression that Davey Stroud was undoubtedly the coach's favourite player in the Kings' squad.

Jane was about to start a conversation with Sam when Danny cleared his throat, clapped his hands and loudly called for silence. 'I've got something to say to everybody but it's specially for Mrs Allenby, our brilliant coach,' he announced in ringing tones. 'Honestly, we couldn't have won the Championship without her. She inspired us, all the guys will tell you that. So, Coach, we want to give YOU something because you've given us loads of good advice and help. This is a thank-you from us to you.'

And, like a conjuror, he produced from behind his back a package wrapped in shiny blue paper with a big white bow. Jane, looking as amazed as she felt, took it from him and to cries of 'Open it! Open it!' from some of the players did as she was told.

'Oh, how wonderful, what a marvellous gift!' she exclaimed as she held up for everyone to see a sweatshirt in the Kings' colours bearing the words: *The World's Best Coach – Kings Rule*. 'I'm overwhelmed, Kings. Thank you, thank you, thank you!' To renewed cheers she pulled Danny towards her and gave him a hug.

'Just shows how much they really appreciate you, Jane,' remarked Sam, rather wishing he'd been given something similar when he coached the Kings. On the other hand, he hadn't won a Championship with them.

'You totally deserve it, Jane,' enthused Taylor Hill, giving her a kiss. 'Oh, and you also know how to *deliver* a good speech, too.'

Jane smiled, knowing that the 'deliver' bit was Taylor's punning reference to her role as a midwife. In the past season she'd had to put up with all manner of jokes about her coaching giving birth to new ideas and delivering promises.

'All the players clubbed together to get it for you,' Danny said. 'Dominic found out your size so it should fit. We want you to wear it to every match. You will, won't you?'

'How can I refuse that request, Danny?' she replied. 'I never imagined you all thought so highly of me, so I'm thrilled.'

After a lot of posing for group and individual photographs, many of them including Sam as well as Jane, players and parents and supporters tucked into the food and drink and talked eagerly about the forthcoming season. Or, in a couple of cases, muttered darkly about the evening's disappointments.

'She really goes for strikers, doesn't she?' Josh confided in the coach's son. 'I mean, why don't defenders get a special award, eh? We do at least as much towards winning a match as the forwards.'

That wasn't a topic Dominic really wanted to discuss. As he believed he wasn't a candidate for awards his interest in the matter was negligible. But he hadn't anyone else to talk to so he had to say something. 'But, Josher, you said as we came here tonight that you consider yourself a striker. I mean, which are you?'

'An all-rounder!' Josh responded promptly. 'And there should definitely be a prize for someone who can play *anywhere* in the team.'

Dominic didn't think there was any reply he could make to that.

Just a few feet away from them Jakki Kelly, mother of Kieren, was having similar thoughts about the lack of reward for defenders. Although she had been completely supportive of Jane during the past season she was beginning to think the coach had eyes only for attackers. Yet, whenever they'd talked about Kieren, Jane had said how much she admired his progress and how much the Kings relied on his slick defending and creative clearances. Unlike most full-backs, he didn't just see it as his job to blast the ball to safety. When clearing his lines he always wanted to find someone to pass to who could make use of the ball. Perhaps Jane needed reminding of that.

Then, before Jakki could manage to get a word with Jane, Sam loomed up at her side and asked how she and Clark, her husband, were getting on. This, Jakki realized, was just the opportunity she needed to promote Kieren's soccer career.

'Did you get much chance of seeing Kieren in action last season, Sam?' she inquired after assuring him that all her family were in excellent health. 'I know you were at Kings' final match but nobody ever judges a player on just one performance, do they?'

'No, you need a chance to do a bit of studying,' Sam agreed. 'Didn't see all that much of Kieren, to be honest, but I was certainly impressed when I did catch him. Coming on well, Jakki.'

'Oh, I'm so glad to hear that, Sam,' she gushed. 'He's very ambitious, you know, and I think he'd really benefit from playing with, well, other top players. You know, county level, at least.'

She paused at that point and watched a grin spread across Sam's face. 'You mean the sort of teams I'm involved in choosing?'

'Oh, well, yes, I suppose so,' she answered, realizing how obvious her motives had been to the former Kings' coach.

'Then I'll bear in mind what you've told me, Jakki,' Sam said quietly. 'Now, I must have a word with Danny, if you'll excuse me.'

When all the celebrations were over and most of the guests had drifted home Jane Allenby at last had time to talk to her son. 'Hardly had a moment for you, have I?' she said apologetically. 'Everybody else seemed to want to talk to me. So, darling, did you enjoy the evening?'

'Was all right, I suppose,' Dominic told her.

'That's not very enthusiastic! Was something wrong?'

He shook his head. 'No, not really. Just, er, thinking about the new season, wondering how we're going to get on.'

'We'll be brilliant again, no doubt about it,' she declared. 'We've still got the same team, haven't we? And I'm sure Davey and Reuben and Danny – oh, and probably Kieren, too – well, they'll simply get better and better. So if we're scoring goals *and* keeping the opposition out we're bound to do well. Don't you agree?'

'Yeah, I expect so,' he replied, though sounding far from convinced. What he couldn't tell her was his own disappointment that she hadn't even mentioned him in her list of players she was relying on to keep the Kings on top. Was that because she no longer rated him? Was that why she hadn't included him in the list of Award winners?

Dominic didn't know the answers to those questions but he was beginning to think that perhaps he'd do much better for himself if he played for a team that wasn't coached by his mother. This, however, wasn't the time to tell her that.

2 *Future Prospects*

Kieren was practising with a tennis ball when his mum craned round the back doorpost and sang out that there was a phone call for him. He'd just managed to bounce the ball from his knee to his shoulder and was trying to hold it in the hollow between the blades. Of course, it fell away as he straightened up. Still, he managed to flick it so accurately with his left foot that it landed in the empty water-tub he'd been using as a target for shooting. It was a good note on which to break off his training on another very warm summer afternoon.

'Who is it?' he asked as he nimbly landed two-footed in the kitchen after imagining that the threshold was an opponent's outstretched leg.

'You'll recognize the voice as soon as you hear the first syllable,' Jakki told him.

He couldn't think what that meant but she was right. 'Foggy! Didn't expect to hear from you. What're you after?'

Foggy Thrale, his former team-mate, got straight to the point. 'You training tonight?'

'Sure. Why, d'you want to join us? Are you wanting to get back into the Kings?'

'No way!' Foggy exploded, the strength of his voice so great that Kieren automatically moved the receiver away from his ear. 'But I want to show you something, something special, after training. Just you, no one else. It's at Uncommon Lane.'

Puzzled, Kieren thought of a problem if he agreed to that. 'But I usually come home with Oats, sometimes with Danny. Just part of the way. Oh yeah, and last week Davey was with us.'

'Well, you're not to bring him with you, not Davey Stroud. He's definitely barred. Just come on your own, that's best. I may let Oats and Danny in on it later.'

'Foggy, what is this? You've got to give me a clue.'

'Can't, mate,' was the brusque response. 'But you won't want to miss out on this,

Kieren, believe me. Could make all the difference to your future as a footballer.'

Kieren really didn't know what to say. The invitation was intriguing, not least because Foggy plainly wanted to exclude at least one of the Kings. And why was he asking him?

'Have you invited anyone else to see this whatever it is, Fogs?' Kieren inquired.

'No, just you. I rate you as a defender, Kieren. Listen, I've got other things to do now so you've got to give me a definite answer, yes or no.'

'OK, then,' he agreed rather reluctantly. 'But I don't want to waste my time after training, so it'd better be good, whatever it is you've got.'

'It will be. OK, then, come over to Cropper's Farm in Uncommon Lane just as soon as you've finished. And don't tell anybody – nobody at all – about this. Promise?'

'Promise,' Kieren agreed.

'See ya,' boomed Foggy, and then the phone went down.

'That sounded very mysterious,' remarked Jakki, who had been doing something inventive to her blonde hair while Kieren had been talking. The wall mirror she was using was within reach of the phone.

'It was,' Kieren agreed again. 'But I can't tell you about it. Can't tell anybody. Foggy made me promise.'

'D'you think he's trying to find a way to rejoin the Kings?' Jakki mused as they returned to the garden where she could resume sun bathing in bikini top and tennis shorts. 'Because he's wasting his time if that's what he wants. Jane was furious with the way he behaved when he couldn't get his own way. He was a very disruptive element, was young Marc.'

'He's probably joined some other team for next season and wants to show me his kit or something,' Kieren suggested. 'Maybe new boots. Fogs always has to boast about *something* he's got.'

But Kieren didn't really believe that and he was still wondering what Foggy wanted as he cycled to the all-weather training pitch at Rodale Kings Leisure Centre where they regularly held their training sessions. He still hadn't decided whether he would go to Cropper's Farm. After all, he suspected that

Foggy had simply invented that bit about his future as a footballer; almost certainly it was one of his old team-mate's typical exaggerations. It might be an idea, first, to try and find out whether Foggy had phoned any other Kings.

The evening was not much cooler than the day and for once even Mrs Allenby was wearing shorts and a T-shirt, a sight that made Kieren realize that she didn't have a figure nearly as good as his mum's. As usual she greeted every boy by name and asked how he was feeling. That wasn't just a pleasantry: they were all under strict orders to tell her if they were feeling unwell in any way or suffering aches or pains from injuries or knocks in recent games for the Kings or any other team or at school. 'Your ability to play well for the Kings depends almost entirely on your physical fitness, so I've got to know if you're not at your best,' she'd told them. 'This is going to be a really testing season for us. We can't afford to go into any game carrying passengers. If you've got problems, tell me. If you conceal them you're in danger of letting the whole squad down.

'Just to ease you into things as gently as possible we'll start with the Boxes,' Jane smiled. 'It'll give our new players a chance to demonstrate what they can do. After that I'm sure things will warm up, probably in every way unless you can make that hot old sun disappear immediately.'

Jane had always been an enthusiast for what she called 'the passing game', arguing that no soccer team ever won anything unless it could pass the ball imaginatively and accurately. In the past she'd even had her players practising that art on a meadow full of bumps and hollows. The Boxes, as she referred to them, were the latest development, whereby a group of five or six players formed a loose circle and passed the ball to one another while two other players within the circle tried to intercept it; and when one of them succeeded he replaced a player forming the circle. The great benefit of this exercise, she explained, was that players were learning how to deliver quick passes from a variety of angles.

Tonight there were enough players to set up two circles. 'It gets to be harder after a

28

while but it can be fun,' Kieren remarked to Harry Greenland, who was joining the Kings as an attacking midfielder, as Jane had described him. Many of the players were wearing just shirts and shorts and trainers and hardly anyone had bothered with socks. So Kieren was interested to see that Harry might well replace him in the squad as the boy with the thinnest legs, a description Kieren disliked. After all, what mattered most was a player's strengths and skills, not his size. In fact, Harry was quite tall, with surprisingly broad shoulders which he hunched when he began one of his threatening runs.

Sean Ferriby, in contrast, was almost as small as Davey with scowling eyes and a liking for darting runs full of jinks and half-circle spins. He brought with him a reputation as a regular goal-scorer at his school, but as none of the other players attended the same school not much was known about Sean; and so far he'd said hardly anything to anyone about himself. One or two of the Kings speculated that Jane had chosen him because he had a passing resemblance, in appearance and style, to Davey Stroud. That hadn't occurred to Davey himself, who so far hadn't formed any opinion at all of someone who might become his rival as a striker. But then, Davey's focus was normally only on his own ability to put the ball in the net.

The box game wasn't kind to Sean. It soon showed that his first touch was weak. Whenever someone hit the ball to him he failed to control it, not once but every single time. Dominic, who was in his group, couldn't resist sending every pass in his direction: and Sean couldn't take them. The ball flicked off his ankles, cannoned away off his knee, spun away from his heel. 'Hey, you're supposed to *return* the ball to someone, not just mess about,' Dominic couldn't help telling him. His mother was in earshot and because she thought someone in the group was fooling about she came across to watch. Sean was sure Dominic had deliberately tried to show him up as a failure. He glowered at him but didn't say anything.

'Sean, go into the middle as an interceptor, switch places with Davey,' the coach ordered. 'Just do your best to get the ball.'

The Kings' newcomer was glad to have

something different to do but he wasn't going to forget Dominic's comment. He knew that normally he could control the ball as well as anyone he played with. It was just that he'd never been asked to do this sort of training at high speed.

Davey always enjoyed taking passes that set him up for goal-scoring chances, especially when they came from his strike partner, Reuben. Happily for him, Reuben was a member of the same group and now they tried to set up a partnership of their own, hitting the ball between them so that none of the others got a chance of a kick. They had no difficulty at all in making sure that Sean couldn't intercept their exchanges, and that further infuriated him. He was convinced they, the whole group, were just having a laugh at his expense.

'Why did you choose him for the Kings, Mum?' Dominic asked Jane during an interval while one of the players scooted away to retrieve the ball after a sliced miskick.

Normally Dominic never commented on any of her decisions as a coach, so the question surprised her. 'Well, he came highly recommended from his previous coach at Greendown,' she answered with her usual directness. 'I've only seen him once in a game and he scored a neat goal – ran on to a pass, swerved past his marker and slotted it very skilfully into the net. Why're you asking?'

Dominic shrugged, not wanting to be accused of interference. 'Just, er, doesn't seem like our kind of player, that's all.'

'Look, you've got to give him a chance,' she said in a low voice as the exercise was about to resume. 'Probably he's still feeling a bit nervous about fitting in with us. He doesn't really know anyone here so it can't be easy for him.'

There was a similar pause for the players who made up the other box and it was then that Kieren had a question for Danny. 'Has Foggy been in touch with you?'

'Foggy? No, what're you on about, KK?'

'Well, I had a mysterious phone call from him. Wants to show me something, he says.'

The goalkeeper laughed. 'Well, he hasn't anything worth showing! You know Foggy, always boasting about something that turns out to be nothing. What else did he say?'

'Wants me to meet him tonight after training, over at Cropper's Farm. Said I could take you with me if I wanted.'

'No way! I'm going off to Oats' place and you know why.'

Kieren sighed. 'So you can get off with his sister, I *imagine*,' he added theatrically. 'Can't imagine what the lovely Andrea sees in you, Danny-boy.'

'You're only jealous because you haven't got a girl,' Danny grinned. 'Hey, that's a thought: maybe Foggy's starting a dating agency and thinks you're someone who should join!'

'Thanks for nothing!' Kieren replied, and then very adroitly trapped the ball that was hit towards him before flicking it up again and hammering a left-foot pass at Harry Greenland.

Danny always enjoyed being an outfield player and at intervals couldn't resist reminding everyone of a spectacular goal he'd scored for the Kings in a Cup Final they'd won. On the other hand, he also liked being in goal and one of his regular complaints was that he didn't get enough practice at shot-saving and catching from set pieces. Jane was quick to assure him that he was brilliant, anyway, and that he was undoubtedly the best keeper in the entire Highlea Sunday League. Danny believed that, too, but he was a perfectionist and so he wanted to ensure that all his skills were always razor-sharp. Hence the need for constantly practising ways of dealing with the unexpected. The truth was, he was happiest when he had a ball in his hands rather than at his feet, in spite of his liking for playing like everyone else.

'Right, time to switch the focus,' Jane told them eventually. 'This is where Danny gets to show off. Practising defending corners and free kicks. We did pretty well last season but I have a feeling teams are getting more sophisticated in this department. Lots of cunning variations, particularly with free kicks. Must be seeing so much top soccer on the telly, I suppose.'

After dividing the squad into attackers and defenders (but with some regular defenders such as Dominic and Josh this time playing as attackers in the hope of varying their skills) she set up a new free-kick routine in which the direction of play was switched twice before a 'free man' darted diagonally towards goal. It took some time for several of the players to get the hang of it and Danny began to get impatient. He still hadn't touched the ball yet.

'Come on, come on, I want to save some shots,' he yelled as Dominic got on the end of one lobbed pass but managed only to balloon the ball high over the bar.

Moments later Danny hadn't the breath even to whisper, let alone shout at anyone. For when Davey managed to weasel his way past static defenders and tried a snap shot Danny went down on his knees to gather the ball. By then, however, Harry Greenland, equally determined to make his mark, had dived in to try to intercept the ball. All he succeeded in doing was stumbling over someone else's foot and then falling very heavily right on top of Danny.

'Sorry, mate,' Harry apologized, scrambling to his feet and then holding out a hand to try and haul Danny upright.

Danny didn't respond. Instead he rolled on to his side, the ball still clutched to his chest and a glazed look in his eyes. Several of the players were starting to make jokes about what they thought was Danny's attempt at humour. Jane, though, recognized at once that her star keeper was in trouble.

'Danny, tell me what's wrong,' she whispered urgently. He was almost gasping for breath and there were tears in his eyes. Gently she prised the ball out of his grasp and then persuaded him to stretch out full-length.

'It's – my – chest,' he was able to tell her at last, his arms now folded tightly over that region.

Jane bit her lip. Her first thought was that Danny might have cracked ribs, a painful injury that took quite some time to heal. If that were the case then she'd need another goalkeeper, at least for the opening matches of the season. Gareth Kingstree, who was Danny's deputy, was really a utility player for almost any role, not a specialist keeper.

'Look, try and stand up, Dan. I mean, your legs are all right, aren't they?'

With her help he got to his feet. All the colour had drained from his face and his appearance now silenced his team-mates.

They, too, were starting to think of how all this was going to affect their coming season. Danny Loxham had always seemed indestructible. Moreover, on the pitch they relied on his exuberant leadership as well as his brilliance in defence. Harry, who hardly knew him at all, was genuinely upset; at heart he was a gentle and thoughtful player who rarely used his size for intimidation. He couldn't help wondering, though, how his new team-mates would feel about him if he'd put the Kings' goalkeeper out of action before the season had started.

Jane knew from her medical training that if it was a fractured rib then it had to be attended to professionally. The lungs could be punctured if sharp, pointed ends were driven inwards. Danny needed to be X-rayed as soon as possible.

'Is it feeling any better?' she inquired after he'd had a few moments to try to regain his normal composure.

'Don't – know,' he puffed, because he didn't. He was in pain and he simply wanted to flop on to the ground. But the coach was making sure she held him up so that he couldn't do any further damage to himself.

'Danny, I'm taking you to hospital,' she told him crisply. 'They'll be able to deal with the problem in no time. Don't worry, you're going to be all right.'

Her goalkeeper nodded once but that was all he could manage for the moment. He wasn't even listening as Jane ordered Dominic to collect any kit Danny had brought with him and put it in her car. The three of them were going off to the hospital together so that meant that training was over for the evening.

'Don't worry about anything, boys, I'm sure everything will be sorted out in double-quick time once I've got Danny to hospital,' she told them. 'If I'd thought there was a serious problem I'd've phoned for an ambulance. Oh, and Harry, don't blame yourself. Accidents are always happening on the football field. You didn't do anything wrong. This was one of those accidents, that's all.'

By the time they were ready to depart in her car, both boys sitting in the back so that Dominic could take care of Danny, the rest of the squad had decided what they were going to do. They all wished Danny the best of luck and now could think of themselves. None of them had any thoughts about continuing with ball work or even kicking into goal.

'How bad d'you reckon it is, Danny's injury?' Gareth Kingstree asked Josh. Although he wasn't often a first choice for the team he certainly didn't fancy the idea of keeping goal every week.

'Can't tell with internal injuries,' replied Josh, who'd had more than his fair share of knocks in recent seasons which allowed him to feel knowledgeable about health matters. 'But he was a funny colour. That tells you a lot.'

'Maybe Mrs Allenby will put you in goal, Josher,' remarked his fellow defender, Frazer McKinnon, usually known as Oats because of his Scottish origin. 'I mean, you said at the Presentation Night that you were an all-rounder, said you could play *anywhere* in the team. So, how about it?'

Josh wasn't sure whether Oats was just winding him up, for he did have a peculiar sense of humour (peculiar, that is, in Josh's opinion). He had no wish whatsoever to play in goal but he didn't like to admit that now. After all, he could do the job at least as well as Gareth.

'Listen, you guys, I've got things to do,' Kieren announced. 'I'm sure Jane will have sorted everything out by next week, even if Danny is out of action for a bit. That's why we voted her Best Coach in the World, right? See you next week then, when the real action begins.'

'Oh, you're not going home my way, then?' Oats asked, looking faintly surprised.

'Er, no. I've got somebody to see. Pretty important, actually.'

Oats nodded his understanding. 'A girl, I suppose.'

'Er, no – well, er, yes,' Kieren floundered, belatedly realizing that a date would be a good cover story for what he was really doing.

'Make your mind up, KK,' Oats responded, grinning widely. 'I think girls must be interested in you. Andrea was asking about you the other day.'

'*Andrea*? Your sister?' Kieren said, now

thoroughly flustered. He knew he was asking an idiotic question but couldn't help himself. 'But, but I thought she was, well, dating Danny. Or, at least, seeing him sometimes.'

The Scottish defender nodded. 'So did I. I know *Danny*'s keen. Well, he hasn't actually said so, but Dan doesn't disguise his feelings very well. Thought she felt the same. But that's girls for you, isn't it? Can't be sure what they're up to.'

'But she definitely wanted to know about me?' Kieren, intrigued, couldn't resist asking for confirmation.

'Aye, I've just said so,' Oats retorted. He was beginning to wish he'd never raised the matter. 'Listen, I must be away. Got plenty to do at home. See you, Kieren.'

'Hey, Oats, don't say anything to her about what we've just been talking about,' Kieren pleaded. 'I'll give her a ring, or call round maybe, tomorrow. OK?'

Frazer was already on the move. He didn't say anything, just nodded, which Kieren recognized could mean anything.

3 Pitch of Dreams

Kieren grabbed his bike and set off for Cropper's Farm, thinking furiously about what he'd just learned. He'd always fancied Andrea, with her blonde ponytail and long legs, but she'd scarcely given him a glance. Even when she raced round the pitch immediately after the Kings won the Championship he wasn't one of the players she rewarded with a spontaneous kiss (naturally, Danny had got one and that had really fired his interest in her following the break-up with Sophie, his then girlfriend). Andrea was a keen footballer herself but so far hadn't managed to get into a team since the family's move from Scotland. Suppose he asked her out and she accepted: how would Danny react to that? Would it cause jealousy and therefore trouble? He'd have to think about it. What didn't occur to him then was that Andrea might be happy to date both him and Danny if she genuinely liked the two of them.

All thoughts about girls and social pleasures went straight out of his head when he arrived at the farm, for the sight that greeted him was amazing. On the far side of the farmhouse a group of four people were hauling a heavy roller over a level stretch of ground – and one of the quartet was Foggy Thrale. That the area was a football pitch couldn't be doubted, for there, at one end, was a set of goalposts complete with net. A *football* field on a farm? That was something Kieren had never heard of, let alone seen.

Because Foggy hadn't noticed his arrival Kieren was able to gaze about him and see that an ancient farm cart was drawn up alongside the near touchline and contained not hay or beet or any other kind of agricultural product but a number of chairs, all of them facing the pitch. Was it intended to be a kind of mini-grandstand? It looked like it to Kieren. The touchline was marked out in glittering white, as was the halfway line and the 18-yard box that constituted the goal area.

Somebody had plainly devoted a great deal of effort to creating an authentic soccer pitch in a most unlikely setting and making it as attractive as possible for prospective players and spectators.

Kieren propped his cycle against a sapling close to the nearest corner of the pitch and that was when Foggy spotted him.

'D'you want to come over and give us a hand?' the former Kings' player boomed.

Kieren shook his head, although he added a grin. 'No thanks. I've done enough hard work for one day. Been training, you know. Tough routines.'

'Don't try and kid me, Kieren! I know the sort of thing you've been up to. None of that compares with what we've been doing here. I mean, we flattened all that land ourselves and then laid out the pitch and all the rest of it. What d'you think?'

'Very impressive,' Kieren admitted after giving the scene another searching look. 'But who's going to play on it? You?'

'Well, of course I am,' answered Foggy, wiping his red-sleeved arm across his round, perspiring face. 'That's what this is all about.

But I won't be on my own, Kieren, no way!'

'I didn't think so,' Kieren replied drily. 'So you're just working out with a bunch of mates? Five-a-sides and so on?'

Foggy didn't reply immediately. He was gathering himself to make an important statement. 'This is going to be the football ground of the future. This is where the top team in the whole of the Highlea District will play. This will be the home of the Giants. But don't ask me the first name because we haven't decided on it yet. We're working on it. And every top player in the area will want to play for us because we'll be the BEST!'

The last word was uttered so loudly that the guys on the roller heard it, even though they were almost at the far end of the pitch. They turned towards Foggy and held thumbs aloft. Foggy waved back.

Kieren frowned. 'You mean, you're hoping to play in a League? But how will you manage that? You can't suddenly join the Highlea Sunday League because it starts next week. They don't admit new teams as fast as that. Oh, and what about new kit for everybody and tracksuits and match balls and stuff like that? Has one of your supporters won the Lottery or the Pools or something?'

'Kieren, my old mate, the secret of success is to plan ahead,' beamed Foggy, doubtless using a phrase he'd rehearsed. 'Our plans are for the season *after* the one that begins next week. By then we'll have *everything* ready. This field is the one where our dreams will come true!'

'Well, that's really something,' Kieren, still blinking, admitted. 'But listen, why d'you want me to know all this? I mean, let's face it, I've never been a particular mate of yours, Foggy, just a team-mate. Why me?'

'Because I reckon you're going to get better and better as a player. I heard old Sam Saxton say that at the Kings' last match when you sneaked the Championship away from Scorton Aces. Well, that's why we want you to come and play for the Giants when we start. We're recruiting you and loads of top players to join me and one or two who're on our side already. You haven't brought Danny with you, have you?'

Kieren shook his head, refraining from trying to be funny by glancing round to see if he'd overlooked Danny's presence. 'Er no, he couldn't get here. Had a bit of a knock during training.'

'Oh well, I'll get in touch with him myself. Thing is, we definitely need a top quality goalie and Danny-boy fills the bill. Honestly, he's wasted with the Kings.'

'You don't fancy any of our strikers, then?' Kieren inquired mildly.

'No way! I'll be the chief striker myself. That's where I should've played with the Kings. I was wasted in midfield, you know that.'

'I don't know that,' was the firm response to that idea. 'I do know that you got sent off against Stonecreek. Jane Allenby said that you didn't want to play for the Kings after she told you you'd let us down. You were just mad with her, weren't you? That's why you walked out on us.'

'OK, I was mad with her, but I was also mad with the referee. I got sent off because I retaliated after that Stonecreek maniac tried to kick holes in me. You'd've been just the same, you'd've wanted to get your own back. Anybody would. But Mrs-Mild-as-Milk

Allenby couldn't see that. Just as she could never see that I was the best in the squad to play centre-forward.'

Kieren had heard enough. He wasn't sorry that Foggy had left the Kings. They could manage very well without his perpetual boasting and low opinion of coaches and team-mates. Although he was fascinated by what he was seeing at Cropper's Farm and hearing of the plans to build a team called the Giants (a typical touch of exaggeration by Foggy, he felt), he'd now had quite enough of his company. He didn't think he'd have the slightest interest in joining a new team in a year's time, especially as it would be under the dictatorial leadership of a boy who was bound to make himself captain.

'Look, I've got to get off. Loads of things to do at home,' he announced, heading for his bike. 'See you around, Fogs.'

'Hey, Kieren, don't say that any more!' Foggy yelled as he put his foot on the pedal.

He paused. 'Don't get you.'

'I'm not *Foggy* here, OK? And I'm not Foggy

with the team I'm playing for this season. I'm Marc. So remember that when we play your lot.'

Kieren delayed his departure for another few moments. '*This* season. I didn't know you were lined up with somebody else. You just talked about the Giants.'

Foggy was beaming again. 'Oh, you don't think I'd miss playing for a whole season, do you? No way! I've been snapped up by Scorton Aces. They were over the moon to get me. Your lot were dead lucky to snatch the Championship from us last season. So we're going to get our revenge when we play you next month. The Aces will *thrash* the Kings. And guess who'll get all the goals for us? Me, Marc Thrale!'

4 Early Setbacks

The sun was still blazing down as the players arrived for the first match of the new season. By now most of them sported tans even if they hadn't left the country for so much as a day during the holidays. Danny Loxham, however, still looked paler than anyone else and that troubled his coach.

'Danny, you will tell me if you feel any pain at all, just the slightest twinge, won't you?' she pleaded as he leaned back against the changing-room wall. 'I know you say you've been all right during training but, well, we all know the difference between that and a real match.'

'Coach, I've told you, I'm *fine*,' her team captain insisted, though she wasn't the only one who thought he sounded a trifle weary. Normally his enthusiasm for everything connected with football shone forth like the sun. 'Those X-rays, they didn't lie, so there's nothing broken. Anyway, goalies are used to a bit of pain. No, I don't mean that: *discomfort*, that's the word, isn't it?'

That was a bit more like him, Jane thought, and smiled. All the same, they'd been told he'd suffered severe bruising in his pre-season collision with Harry Greenland and that always took time to heal. Jane had been in two minds about whether to play him against Torridon today but, really, there was no one else she could trust to take his place. She hadn't signed a second goalkeeper during the close season to strengthen the squad and that was an error. Now, unless a team suffered a real emergency or lost the services of a squad member, the League wouldn't allow further signings. She would have liked to discuss the situation with another coach but that would have been an admission to a rival that the Kings had a worrying weakness. It hadn't occurred to her that Sam Saxton was a man she could have consulted without the risk of giving away vital information.

'Well, don't try to be too brave,' she told Danny as she put a hand on his shoulder to underline her acceptance of his point of view. 'We don't want to lose the best keeper in the League, do we?'

She couldn't help wondering whether he was as fit as he claimed to be. His skin was very warm to the touch for, like the rest of the players, he hadn't yet put a shirt on: or, in his case, his multi-coloured goalkeeper's jersey. But, she decided, as with most problems time would tell whether it was bad or simply imaginary.

She herself was feeling particularly over-heated because she was wearing the 'Best Coach in the World' sweatshirt and she could hardly take it off now. It had seemed the right occasion to put it on to demonstrate that she was genuinely pleased with the squad's celebratory gift. On the other hand, its very boastfulness made her feel self-conscious about it. After all, strangers might very well think she'd chosen it for herself.

Perhaps, she reflected, she could wear something else in future now they'd seen she appreciated their tribute. There was always the excuse that it was 'in the wash', a statement even Dominic wouldn't be likely to dispute.

'I know you don't remember most of what I say just before the kick-off, Kings,' she declared, raising her voice to catch their attention. Rather to her surprise the noise level dropped immediately and some of those putting on shirts or shorts actually paused. Somehow, they'd sensed that this was an important message. She smiled. Perhaps she and her players were now completely in tune all the time. 'This is really important because it's nothing to do with tactics or attitudes, it's all about health – *your* health.'

Every pair of eyes was focused on her as she added: 'On days as hot as this it's easy to get dehydrated. You'll all sweat a lot and if you don't replace some of that fluid you'll suffer, and so will the team's performance. So if you start to feel dry-mouthed or a bit woozy or anything like that then come and get a drink. We've got a good supply of that energy drink you all like. So if you need it, *drink* it. Understand?'

'Yes, Coach,' several of them chorused, as they liked to do when they were being asked a question that wasn't a problem for any of them.

'OK, good. Last thing: remember we're the champions. So play like champions – and behave like champions. I don't want any red or yellow cards, thank you. It would be good to win the Clean Play Award this season wherever we finish in the League table.'

She didn't want to make too much of that but she'd become concerned at the decline in playing standards, caused, she was convinced, by those youngsters who felt they had to imitate some of the worst habits of the adult players they saw in televised matches. It needed to be eradicated as soon as possible. Yet she suspected that if she tried to make a big thing of it, perhaps during or after a training session, some of the squad might be so eager to follow her requirements that they would pull out of tackles or hesitate to try to win the ball in fifty–fifty situations. Thus they'd just hand the initiative to the opposition. She didn't want that, naturally. She desperately wanted to win the Championship again, if only to prove that the first time wasn't a fluke or beginner's luck. So she'd have to do more thinking about how to get her message across.

Torridon looked to be a side just as fit and eager as her own. She liked their strip of white shirts with a diagonal red stripe and red shorts. It was while she was admiring it that she realized she knew one of their players, actually knew him quite well. Alex Todd, the slim, dark-haired striker she'd last seen playing for the Kings. But that was a couple of seasons ago when his father, Ricky Todd, was her predecessor as coach. Alex had lots of skills but was inclined to sulk if anything went against him. Indeed, that was why he left the Kings: he had walked out after his father dropped him because of his loss of form.

Strange, that, she found herself thinking, for Marc Thrale had also walked out in a huff after she had criticized his lack of discipline following a sending-off last season. Quickly she ran her eye over the Torridon players on the pitch but no, Foggy wasn't among them. In a way that was a relief: she knew she wouldn't enjoy the *two* former Kings combining and, probably, conspiring to defeat their old team.

Nobody had mentioned Alex's change of

club so perhaps none of the present Kings had known they'd be facing him today. Well, doubtless they'd welcome him back on to the same pitch in their own way! She glanced along the touchline but there was no sign of Ricky Todd. Although she saw him in Rodale village from time to time they'd not spoken beyond the usual pleasantries and she supposed his interest in football had waned after he'd given up coaching.

'Well, you're not leaving us in any doubt about how you regard yourself, are you, Jane?' someone greeted her. She'd been so lost in her own thoughts that she hadn't noticed Dane Credland come up to shake hands.

'Oh, hello, Dane, sorry I didn't notice you,' she responded, aware that Torridon's coach was eyeing the slogan on her shirt. 'Yes, I'm afraid it is a bit over the top, but the shirt was a gift from the boys. Don't know how they managed to save up for it!'

Dane just nodded politely but Jane suspected he didn't entirely believe her explanation. He was someone she saw quite often, as he worked in a Rodale building-society branch where she had an account, but they never talked football on those occasions. She rather thought that he might not approve of female coaches.

'I've just noticed that you've got one of our former players in your team; Alex Todd,' she remarked to be friendly. 'How's he playing these days?'

'Seems to be settling in well. We only got him towards the end of last season. I'm sure he'll want to make a big impression today. Anyway, must get back to the team. Hope you have a good season, *after* today!'

The opening match of the new season had attracted a very good crowd. Among the spectators were several young girls wearing blue shorts similar to the Kings' and it was obvious from their cheering and squeals of delight that they were practically a fan club in themselves. Jane noticed Andrea McKinnon, Frazer's sister. She must remember to ask if she'd found a team to play for because Andrea had let it be known that she was keen to play soccer herself, though she didn't like the idea of being in a girls-only side. A newspaper photographer was taking pictures of both teams and Jane was thankful he hadn't wanted to include her. It really would be embarrassing to be seen in that sweatshirt by every reader.

Danny won the toss and automatically chose to play towards the cricket pavilion end, always a favourite ploy. Nobody had kept a record of how many games it might have helped them to win but by now all the established players felt it brought them luck.

'Must be a good omen,' smiled Jakki Kelly as she came to stand beside Jane. She hoped it showed that she knew as much about the Kings as anyone. 'We really need to start a new campaign on a winning note, don't we?'

That was so obvious that Jane didn't bother to reply. Her attention was on Dominic and Alex Todd. The former team-mates were holding an intense-looking conversation and Jane hoped it wasn't full of threats and silly boasts.

Normally her son was calm in almost every situation but she could imagine that Alex would be in the mood to wind him up. Each would want to put one over the other; that was perfectly natural. Just as long as it didn't lead to undue aggression and the referee flourishing yellow or red cards. Jane would have to get a message to Dominic not to allow himself to be provoked.

Alex was on the move from the kick-off, swinging the ball out to a team-mate on the right wing and darting through the centre in the hope of a quick return pass. It didn't come his way then but before long he had the ball again, neatly turned Dominic with a clever side-foot movement and then hit an excellently weighted pass to his co-striker, William Horleigh, out on the right. When the cross came in it was Alex who got on the end of it, jumping well to try a snap header that was aimed at the top corner of the net. To Jane's relief Danny got across to it and tipped the ball over the bar for a corner.

Torridon's supporters were already vocal and yells of 'Come on the Dons!' were reaching a climax as the ball swung into the crowded penalty area. This time Kieren got his head to it first but the clearance was feeble. Back in it went and William Horleigh managed a half-volley that led to a fierce scramble when Frazer miskicked. Someone else appeared to handle the ball and the appeals for a penalty were heated and frantic. The ref just waved play on. Dominic took the opportunity to blast the ball as far as he could and, for the moment, the siege of the Kings' goal was over.

'Phew, that was a bit sticky,' gasped Jakki. 'Would have been terrible if we'd gone a goal down in the very first minute of the new season!'

Once again, Jane didn't think she needed to make a verbal response to such a banal comment. What she wanted to say was that the trouble had really been caused by Kieren's weak header but that would only have annoyed or even upset Jakki. Best to say nothing, sometimes.

Torridon had clearly found their touch right away. After swatting away Rodale's first attack when Davey's first touch let him down they resumed their offensive and began to batter the Kings' defence mercilessly. Thrice more within minutes defenders conceded corners. Although not the tallest of strikers, Alex Todd had always managed to soar when he needed to, partly as a result of his rhythmical training exercises on his toes. His timing was excellent. On the two occasions he headed for goal he was thwarted once by the woodwork and the second time by an unlucky deflection from the in-rushing William's left shoulder.

'You'll never score against me, Toddy!' Danny jeered as the players took their swiftly changing places for yet another corner kick.

'You just watch me, Loxham,' Alex retaliated. 'We're the team going to the top this season, no danger.'

Somehow, though, Rodale Goal Kings held out against all forms of attack. No one was playing better than Kieren Kelly. Following his initial poor clearance he hadn't put a foot wrong and his positive tackles and timely interceptions were among the causes of the Dons' frustration. Reuben Jones had been dropping ever deeper to help the beleaguered defenders but as a result the service to Davey and Larry, Kings' strikers, was negligible.

Then, completely against the run of play, the Kings took the lead. Kieren initiated the move with a long run out of defence. With the opposition back-pedalling because they expected this back-line defender to pass to someone Kieren went a long way before he met any resistance. Then, looking up, he swung the ball as far as he could across the pitch to Lloyd Colmer, a bustling, ever enthusiastic midfielder who'd run hard in the hope of getting a pass. Torridon's keeper advanced towards the right of his box, confident that the boy with the mass of tightly curled black hair would pass to the big, rather awkward looking striker on his inside. Instead, Lloyd ignored Larry Hill completely and fed Davey Stroud with an absolute gem of a long-distance pass.

Although Davey had been on the point of signalling that he wanted the ball it hadn't really seemed likely that he'd get it. Davey, though, was usually prepared for anything: which was why he scored so many instinctive goals. This time he pulled the ball down with his left foot, swivelled to his right to elude an on-rushing opponent, swung to his left for just two strides and then, with his left foot again, lofted the ball diagonally across the penalty area into the unprotected net. The goalkeeper was still rushing across to cut off the shot as the ball went past him, high over his right shoulder.

'Oh yes! Great goal, Davey!' Jane exulted, hands high above her head to applaud him.

'Kings Rule! Kings Rule!' chanted their squadron of fans.

Torridon's supporters simply looked stunned, as they had every right to do. After being battered ceaselessly practically since the match began Rodale Goal Kings had taken the lead in their very first attack. How on earth had they done it? Basically, with just two precision passes and the flair of an outstanding goal-scorer. Was that how a team became champions?

No one was more aghast than Alex Todd. For some moments he stood on the edge of the centre circle simply shaking his head in disbelief. Then his face darkened as he swung round to glare at the grinning goal-scorer. 'That was just a fluke, that shot. You'd never do that again in a hundred years, Stroud!'

The grin didn't disappear. 'Just watch me, Alex,' was Davey's ironical use of Alex's own phrase.

'Don't get heated, boys,' warned the referee after a glance at the Torridon striker's expression. 'I don't tolerate bad behaviour. Remember that.'

Inevitably, the Dons replied immediately with a flurry of raids from practically all directions. Having soaked up so much pressure already, the Kings' defence was able to withstand the new assaults reasonably comfortably.

Dominic Allenby was in commanding form and Alex kept venturing to the flanks in the hope of drawing the central defender out of position. Dominic wasn't tempted. Reuben, who'd seen Alex in action on other occasions and knew he was a potent threat wherever he played, had decided to shadow the ex-Kings' striker. That wasn't what Mrs Allenby wanted from him but she couldn't attract his attention to give him fresh instructions.

'That was a marvellous goal from Davey, wasn't it?' remarked Jakki Kelly, coming in to stand beside the coach.

'Certainly was!' Jane agreed. 'I'm just amazed we've scored at all with the way Torridon have been pounding our defence. Can hardly believe we've taken the lead.'

'You saw how it started, didn't you?' Jakki continued.

'Oh yes. That long cross-field pass from Lloyd. Excellent vision! Just what I've been telling –'

'No, no, before that, Jane. It was Kieren who brought the ball out, beat everybody, *then* passed to Lloyd. I mean, that was the pass that set everything up.'

Jane glanced at her companion's expression. There was no doubt that Kieren's mother regarded that pass as the equal of Davey's scoring shot. 'Er, yes, it did. You know, I'm so pleased Davey scored our first goal of the season because, of course, he scored the last one of last season. Sort of joins things together rather neatly, doesn't it?'

Almost as soon as she said that she knew it was a mistake. She shouldn't have switched the attention away so quickly from what Jakki clearly saw as Kieren's moment of glory. But before she had a chance to make amends, she was needed on the pitch.

Frazer McKinnon had gone down under a charging tackle from a Torridon midfielder and the ref was signalling for medical assistance. As Jane grabbed her treatment bag and dashed towards her stricken player the ref was lecturing the offender before flourishing a yellow card.

Oats had already rolled down his sock to reveal an ugly scrape on the back of his calf that extended almost to the heel. Blood was seeping from the wound and the victim was in a lot of pain. Tenderly Jane cleaned the wound and then started to apply protective covering. She doubted that he needed stitches, fortunately. The referee was peering at her handiwork and shooting glances at his watch.

'Really, he should be off the pitch, you know,' he remarked testily. 'You'll be substituting him, won't you?'

'I expect so,' replied Jane, surprised by the question. Was this ref wanting to do her job for her?

'How d'you feel now, Frazer?' she inquired as she cradled his leg in her hands, waiting for the pain-killing spray to take effect.

'It's a wee bit, er, painful,' he admitted, which she guessed should have been 'very painful'.

'Well, I'm taking you off, putting Harry on in your place,' she told him. 'I don't want you to risk further damage today.'

'OK,' he said, still grimacing. That alone told her how much he was suffering. Not one of her players ever wanted to come off voluntarily. Dominic had once told her that every player feared that if he was substituted then he might never get his place back again because his replacement kept on playing brilliantly.

All the same, Oats declined an offer to be carried off physically by two of his teammates and instead managed to hop to the touchline with just Jane's shoulder for support. After telling Harry Greenland that he was to take Frazer's place, and how she wanted him to play, she glanced down the line of spectators to see if she could spot the long, fair hair of Sallie McKinnon, Frazer's mum. With no sign of her being present Jane had a word with Andrea.

'Please keep an eye on your brother, Andrea, and let me know if he needs any help,' she requested. 'Is your mum giving you a lift home after the match?'

'Not sure. Said she wanted to catch up on some letter-writing this morning. Oh, and she's researching an article for a magazine at home – you know, in Scotland.'

'Frazer, rest your leg as much as you can,' his coach ordered. 'If you don't get a lift after the match I'll take you home myself. You're not to walk unnecessarily today. OK?'

When, at last, she was able to turn her attention back to the match she was just in time to see the Kings suffer their next setback. Harry was clumsy in his attempt to control a ball that had bounced higher than he expected on the concrete-hard pitch. As he waited to make a second try William Horleigh, darting in, took the ball at ankle-height, swerved past another defender and then hit a rocket of a shot towards the top of the net. Danny, not expecting any shot at all from that distance, was slow to move. Even if he had reacted faster it was doubtful whether he'd've been able to reach the ball before it hit the rigging by the rear stanchion.

With what proved to be the last kick of the ball before the half-time whistle shrilled Torridon had equalized.

It was impossible for Harry to look any glummer when he came face to face with the Kings' coach. 'Sorry, bad mistake,' he mumbled, horrified by the thought that he'd given a goal away with what amounted to his first kick in Rodale's purple-and-white colours.

'It was bad, but you've got to get over it, Harry,' Jane told him briskly. 'Don't keep thinking about it when you get back on the pitch. Just concentrate on winning the ball. Remember that at this level opponents can have fast reactions. Be alert to who's around you all the time.'

She turned to Reuben and told him she didn't want him sticking to Alex Todd like a shadow. 'The defence can do that job. I want you in midfield, providing a service for Davey and Larry, joining up with them if the right opening is there. We're creating nothing in attack.'

She had a few more points to make and they mostly listened attentively. They knew they hadn't played well. OK, Torridon were better than they expected, but Kings were the champions, not the opposition. 'So go out now and play like champions. Don't let Torridon boss you about. Rule!'

They returned to action with a more determined look on their faces. So, too, did the Torridon players. After all, they had the inspiration of a late equalizer. Dane Credland had told them they were so much better than the opposition they ought to be leading by at least three clear goals and they wanted to show they believed him. Within moments they were attacking again. When the ball was whipped across to Alex on the edge of the box he took a snap shot. Danny was able only to finger-tip the ball against an upright and from there Kieren headed it to safety at the expense of a corner.

'Go on, Toddy, get your own back!' a voice boomed from behind Danny's goal and probably most people at the match heard it.

'Foggy!' exclaimed everyone who knew him.

Jane frowned. She hadn't been aware that he was present and perhaps he had arrived only at half-time. It saddened her that a former player should show such hostility to his old team-mates; and demonstrate it so publicly. It had been his own decision to leave the Kings, although Jane knew she wouldn't have wanted him to stay.

Whether Foggy's presence made any difference to Danny she didn't know, but the goalie made a hash of dealing with the ball when it came over. His attempt to punch it as hard as possible misfired. He succeeded only in fisting it towards Kieren who managed to head it out only by twisting his neck right round. It didn't go far, either. A Torridon defender hoisted it back into the box, there was a fierce scramble for possession, the ball ricocheted back from the base of a post – and, infuriatingly, there was Alex Todd to back-heel it into the net.

'Yes! Great goal, Alex Todd!' Foggy roared.

It was nothing of the sort. But Alex was happy to accept that version. 'Told you, Loxham, told you!' he exulted before dashing out of the box, arms held high, fists clenching and shaking. He continued his run to receive a hug from his coach and to smirk at Jane Allenby. She was sure he was going to say something to her but, sensibly, he didn't. Actions for him had already spoken louder than words.

It was a sickening blow for all sorts of reasons and for the moment Jane couldn't think what else she could do to try to repair the damage. For some reason the team simply weren't functioning as a unit, as they had done the previous season during their clinching run to the title. They had allowed Torridon to dominate the game from the outset and even Davey's goal had failed to lift them. *Something* had to be done without delay or victory would be beyond them.

5 Settling a Score

Torridon didn't sit back on their lead. One goal certainly wasn't enough for Alex Todd and he couldn't imagine anything better in life than scoring a hat-trick against his former team-mates. His revenge for the way he'd been treated, he believed, would be complete. By now he'd begun to overlook the fact that his real difference of opinion had been with his father, Ricky, then the Kings' coach.

Now, as he waited for the ball to reach him again, he couldn't help glancing around the ground to see if his father was present. That was a faint hope, really, because Ricky Todd had more or less abandoned football after surrendering his coaching role to Jane Allenby at the time he sold his factory in Rodale to a foreign company. He had taken up golf and his Sundays were spent pursuing a small white ball, not watching a football.

As she wrestled with the problem of what to do for the best Jane, too, thought of Ricky and couldn't help checking to see whether her predecessor was present. Thankfully, she couldn't spot him but she noted that Sam Saxton had turned up and, at that moment, was in conversation with Jakki Kelly. A sudden thought struck the Kings' coach: was Jakki asking Sam if he was interested in taking charge of the Kings again? As a parent of one of the players and a member of the Friends of Rodale Kings Committee Jakki probably felt entitled to make such a move. A former lead singer in a rock group, Jakki was very positive in everything she did; and there was no doubt that she wanted Kieren to reach the top as a footballer.

The next blunder on the pitch was committed by Dominic. Trying to win the ball in a tussle with William Horleigh near the by-line, Dominic sensed he was about to lose his balance, put out a hand to save himself and succeeded only in pushing his opponent to the ground; and the ball ran over the line for a corner kick. Instead of regarding the whole thing as just a clumsy tackle the ref blew furiously, whipped out a yellow card and booked Dominic for a foul. When the Kings' central defender protested he was merely trying to save himself from a fall the ref curtly told him to be quiet or suffer a worse penalty.

To his credit, William didn't make any fuss about the incident or try to claim that he'd been hurt in the tumble. He simply made the most of it by scoring the goal which came about as a direct result of a well-flighted corner kick. When the ball came swinging over Torridon's tallest defender rose above everyone and nodded it sideways towards William, who had no trouble at all in steering it into the net.

'Where *were* you, Danny?' Jane wailed, although she managed to ask that question inwardly. He really should have been able to reach that ball ahead of everyone. Instead, he'd tried to punch it clear and missed the ball completely.

Not everyone present who supported the Kings could remain silent.

'Come on, Kings, what're you doing? You're playing like chumps, not champs!' a female voice yelled.

Jane couldn't identify the voice and, when she looked along the touchline, couldn't tell who'd been calling out. *Chumps* was a word she hadn't heard for years and yet she wouldn't deny that it fitted. It hardened her resolve to do something about the troubles on the pitch. First, she'd go and have a word with Danny. As she marched purposefully round the playing area she was aware of many glances at her sweatshirt. Some must have wondered why she was wearing one at all on such a sultry day but most were reading the declaration about the best coach. And doubtless most of *them* would be thinking she hardly deserved it with her team playing so badly. So, just before she reached the back of the net Danny was guarding, she took it off and tied it round her waist.

'Sorry about that mistake, Coach,' Danny apologized before she could say a word. He knew why she was there and his grey eyes really were full of remorse.

'Why are you trying to punch the ball all the time instead of catching it?' she wanted to know. 'Are you just trying to practise for your boxing training?'

'No, no,' he replied. She'd touched on something that was at least partly true but he couldn't admit it. 'Just seemed the best way of getting rid of the ball. I couldn't reach it properly because Kieren was in my way.'

Jane hadn't seen that and suspected Danny was finding an easy excuse. She switched to something else. 'You haven't been talking to your team-mates much, have you? We're going through a bad spell at present and I think they need your leadership. You should be shouting encouragement, Danny.'

'Sorry,' he said – and then had to dash out of goal to clear a back-pass from Dominic, who was making sure Alex couldn't get the ball. As the ball soared back towards the half-way line Jane reflected that at least Danny's kicking was still straight and strong. All the same, he didn't seem to be quite the player he was last season.

The moment he'd cleared the ball Danny turned his attention again to the supporters on the touchline. Andrea had now deserted her brother, who was lying on the ground but propping himself up on an elbow to keep an eye on the play. Andrea had rejoined the other girls and Danny stared at them avidly. There was no doubt that Andrea looked stunning in shorts. Even Sophie, the girl who'd so cruelly rejected him, hadn't a figure as good as Andrea's. It was time to take their relationship a step or two further, he was sure. He must think of something to take her to that would be irresistible, something completely different from the swimming party he'd invited her to and which, after a week of keeping him waiting for an answer, she'd turned down.

With a 3–1 lead Torridon were beginning to think they'd done more than enough to win the match; in the sweltering conditions some of the players were plainly wilting. Dane Credland was on the point of making his first substitution, simply to rest tired legs, when one of his centre-backs lunged into Davey Stroud as the Kings mounted a rare raid. Davey stumbled over the ball, lost his balance, tried desperately to recover it but couldn't. He fell flat on his face.

The piercing note of the ref's whistle claimed everyone's attention.

'Oh, no!' the Torridon coach wailed as he saw that the official was pointing, with rather unnecessary emphasis, to the penalty spot. Even though his team had a two-goal lead Dane knew very well the difference one goal could make to a side trying to catch up. Moreover, the Kings hadn't become champions without proving how resilient they could be in adversity.

Davey was the Kings' penalty-taker and it was his spot-kick that had effectively won them the Championship in that final game of the previous season. As people had observed, he seemed to possess no nerves at all when about to take the kick that could change their fortunes in any game.

Yet, when he picked himself up now, he felt strangely tired. He couldn't say why that was even though he'd been on the move virtually non-stop throughout the game, eager for any half-chance to attack. He was used to demonstrating that he had seemingly inexhaustible energy.

This time his left-foot shot lacked his customary power and precision. The goalie guessed correctly that his aim would be low to his own right and that's the way he went. He saved with ease and his co-defenders descended on him jubilantly.

Jane groaned to herself as Davey, shoulders hunched, paused and then turned away in dismay. They weren't alone in realizing that that was the end of the match for the Kings. They'd started the defence of their Championship with a humiliating home defeat, humiliating because they'd performed so poorly throughout the game and made many uncharacteristic errors.

'I'm sure you won't play so badly again this season,' Dane Credland told Jane graciously at the final whistle. 'I'm just pleased it was us you were playing today.'

'Thanks, Dane,' she replied, shaking his hand. 'Congratulations on your win. You deserved it.'

'Sorry about missing the penalty, Coach – don't know what went wrong,' apologized Davey the moment he left the pitch. He looked devastated and, beneath his suntan, he appeared quite pale, as if he'd suffered a real shock. Suddenly, Jane guessed the cause.

'Davey, have you had any of the energy drink during the match?'

'Er, no, Coach, I forgot,' he confessed. 'Didn't think I needed it.'

'Well, drink this now. Go on, you *do* need it.'

Davey obeyed. Jane knew she had no right to be cross with him. She was the one at fault. It was her job to see that the players kept fit by following her instructions. In what was, literally, the heat of the match it was all too easy to forget everything as they strove to put the ball in the net. Three or four other players followed Davey's lead and thankfully swallowed the reviving drink. None looked anything but miserable as they trooped, heads down, to the changing-room. A few spectators clapped half-heartedly and murmured sympathetic words. Every home supporter had supposed the Kings would start the defence of their title with a crushing victory so it was hard to accept they'd been defeated so easily.

'Maybe they were just over-confident,' remarked Jakki to Sam as they studied the disconsolate Kings. 'I mean, that can easily happen at their age. Still, I'm sure Jane will know how to get them back on the winning track. It would be disastrous, wouldn't it, if they lost their next match as well?'

In fact, Jane was far from sure that she even knew the reason for the Kings' poor performance against Torridon, a team she considered to be nowhere near as good as her own. It couldn't be lack of fitness, for the Kings had shown great enthusiasm for their pre-season training and, what's more, several of the players also had their own routines for building up their strength as well as their skills. It most certainly wasn't lack of ambition: Danny and his team-mates were just as keen to hold on to their Championship as she was. So, it had to be something *she* was responsible for: the make-up of the team she'd put out today or her choice of tactics. What was it she'd done wrong? As she followed the boys into the changing-room she had no idea at all how to answer that question.

Danny hadn't gone with the rest of them: moments after the final whistle sounded he darted across the pitch to where Oats was being watched by his sister as he walked round in a circle, testing his injured leg.

'How is it, Oats?' he inquired, although he was really looking at Andrea.

'Still hurts a wee bit but I suppose I'll

survive,' Frazer replied stoically. 'Wish I'd got my own back on the guy who did it, though.'

'You'd feel better if the Kings had won,' Andrea remarked sharply. 'Danny, you had a terrible game. What were you thinking about when you let them score?'

That comment shocked him. He hadn't been aware she was taking so much interest in the match. Sophie, his previous girlfriend, displayed no interest in football whatsoever.

'Er, it was, well, just a mistake, that's all,' he managed to come up with as her beautiful dark brown eyes bored into him. 'I mean, everyone makes mistakes, don't they?'

'Goalkeepers can't afford to,' she replied unanswerably.

Danny glanced at Oats, wishing his team-mate would take himself out of earshot for a few moments. 'Er, can I have a private word, Andrea?' he asked tentatively.

'No,' was the immediate response. 'Big brother here needs me to nurse him back to health. But you can give me a ring tonight if you like. I can take the phone to my own room so that'll be perfectly private. OK?'

He was content with that. It was even an

exciting prospect, knowing that she'd *invited* him to ring her. By that time he'd have come up with some idea of where they could go on a date.

'Fine,' he said as casually as he could manage. 'Get yourself fit quickly, Oats. We'll need you for the Greendown game. See ya, then.'

He couldn't resist a backward glance as he left them, but his focus was not on Frazer's limp but on Andrea's bare legs and blonde hair.

The rest of the Kings' squad was still in the changing-room when he got there and most of them were still in their playing kit. To his surprise, Jane Allenby was also present, for normally she left them on their own after a match unless she had to attend to someone's injury. Everyone still looked solemn but that was understandable.

'Danny, I'm glad you've joined us,' the coach greeted him. That made him wonder whether she was mad with him but keeping her temper for the moment. So he was glad she didn't ask him what he'd been doing since the final whistle. He tried a smile and offered no explanation.

'We're having an immediate inquest because I can't remember us playing so badly,' she went on. 'We need to know why it all went wrong. So, can you think of any reason?'

Most heads had already turned towards him. Had they offered any ideas? Danny really didn't know what to say but he supposed something was necessary. After all, he was captain.

'We didn't score enough goals,' he said, thinking that a touch of humour might improve the atmosphere in the room.

'Look, I know I missed a penalty, but that's not fair!' Davey said quite fiercely. 'I didn't get many other chances, you know. You didn't either, did you, Hilly?'

Larry Hill looked startled to be included in Davey's denial but didn't say anything. He knew he'd contributed almost nothing to the match. The previous day he'd been sick after a meal and whether it was the after-effects of that or the heat of the morning he simply hadn't felt very well. Larry knew, though, that excuses of that kind were not worth putting forward to explain poor play. His team-mates could be merciless in mocking any player who said the wrong thing at the wrong moment. So he just shrugged.

'Well, *of course*, we didn't score enough goals, the result proves that,' Jane pointed out. 'I was hoping we might dig a little deeper for the reasons. Reuben, have you got any thoughts?'

The fair-haired playmaker had anticipated the question and tried to come up with a convincing answer, although he was sure it wasn't the whole truth. 'Well, they seemed to be a lot quicker than us, Coach. They were really up for this match. Maybe because we're the champions. I mean, they'd be *desperate* to start the season with a win against the champions, wouldn't they? So they were really buzzing, put our defence under loads of pressure.'

He paused because he thought he'd probably said enough, but Jane was nodding eagerly. 'Good thinking, Reuben. But keep going, if you can. I want as many opinions as possible.'

Encouraged, Reuben continued: 'Well, you see, that's why I kept dropping back to mark the boy who used to play for you – us, I mean.

Yeah, Alex Todd. He was always dangerous. Like I said, he'd be desperate to beat us just on his own. So, anyway, I thought the defence needed strengthening. Sorry you felt I wasn't doing my real job, setting up chances and stuff.'

Before Jane could explain what he meant Dominic joined in. 'I agree with you, Lefty. I think we were a bit slow today. Know I was. But don't know why. Maybe we all had the idea that Torridon would be easy because we beat them last time. Different season, different team. That's how I see it.'

Jane almost wished he hadn't said all that because so much of it was what she felt. Yet if she said that now the rest of the Kings might just feel that it was the sort of coach-and-son alliance they'd been assured many times didn't exist. It surprised her that he'd spoken at all because usually he kept silent when team matters were under discussion in case anyone got the wrong impression. His comments now indicated how strong his feelings were.

'*I* don't think our defence was slow today,' Kieren counter-attacked. 'I know I wasn't. You weren't either, Josher, were you?'

Josh Rowley blinked with surprise. 'Er, no. No, definitely not. Maybe we got caught out of position once or twice. But that's all. Oh, and –'

'You mean me, don't you?' Danny cut in. 'Well, nobody's perfect. I made one or two little mistakes but I don't usually. You all know that.'

'Listen, it was only one defeat, just three points dropped, that's all,' Kieren went on. 'We'll soon get back to our usual level. We'll still bash the hell out of the rest of the League.'

Jane was a little startled. Kieren had a point: it *was* just one defeat and every team was bound to lose at least once during the season. Did it really matter whether that loss came in the first game or the fifteenth? In terms of points at stake the answer had to be no. On the other hand, psychologically it was a severe blow to their pride to be outwitted so easily in the first game of the season on their own pitch.

'Kieren, you're right, of course,' she acknowledged quickly. 'It's just the *way* in which we lost that really worries me. You weren't the real Kings out there today, more like imposters dressed up in royal clothing!'

She smiled but no one laughed. Davey, for one, was still unhappy with the way Jane had failed to appreciate the point he made about poor service. If strikers didn't get a supply of the ball then they couldn't score, could they? And today the midfield had been non-existent. So, come to that, had Larry Hill. Should he suggest changes while everyone was present or wait until he could have a word with Mrs Allenby on his own? Perhaps best to get it done now. As the holder of the Player-of-the-Season Award he surely had some authority in the squad.

'That was a great pass from Lloyd that I got for the goal I scored,' he said, having decided to begin with praise. 'But we weren't getting much service apart from that. Can't do everything on my own. And yeah, before anyone says it, I know I got the Player-of-the-Season Award and so I'm supposed to be good.'

One or two eyebrows went up on hearing that but no one backed him up or tried to make a joke of it. Larry, however, looked distinctly uneasy. He felt he had to defend his role.

'Look, I'm up there, too, Davey. I want to get the ball in the net as well,' he pointed out in a fairly hesitant manner.

'Yeah, I know,' was Davey's cool response. His listeners, especially Larry, could make what they wanted of that comment.

Sensing that if she wasn't careful opinions might become spiteful or damaging, Jane decided enough was enough. Plainly there were different views about what, or more likely who, could be blamed for the defeat. That was something she'd have to think about and possibly discuss with individual players before the next match against Greendown a week later. At this moment she couldn't tell whether anything had been achieved or actually made worse by this post-match inquest.

'Look, we'll stop there and –' she was starting to say when Harry Greenland intervened to ask if he could say something.

'Of course you can, Harry. You're just as entitled to your opinion as anyone else. Just because you're a newcomer doesn't mean you're not part of the squad. With your fresh eyes you could've noticed something the rest of us have been overlooking for ages.'

'Thanks,' he said, with a nod in her direction. 'Well, I know I made a mistake when I let an opponent get past me and score the equalizer. But I haven't got eyes in the back of my head. I couldn't see him where he was. But if someone had *warned* me he was there maybe I'd've been able to do something about him. And Danny could've done with someone putting him in the picture when he was – what's the word? – unsighted right after that free kick early in the second half.' Harry paused, took a breath and went on: 'All I'm saying, you guys, is that we ought to talk to each other more when it helps the man on the ball. I know it worked for us in my old team. Oh, and it definitely was a big help to me loads of times when I was in goal.'

Jane was nodding her full approval of what he was saying long before his final words. They were a real surprise and she had to know more. 'Harry, I'd no idea you'd been a goalkeeper. That wasn't for your last team, was it?'

He shook his head. 'No, the one before that. And I played in goal quite a lot when I was at my primary school.'

'Why'd you give it up then?' inquired Danny, who had been brooding on his teammate's views on defenders talking to each other. Had Jane persuaded Harry to speak like that to reinforce her own remarks to him towards the end of the match?

'I wanted to get into the game more,' was the unexpected reply from the Kings' newest central defender. 'We had a pretty good team and didn't concede many goals. I got bored between the posts. So I got the coach to give me a chance in defence. I liked it and he liked what I did. Simple!'

'Well, Harry that could be very good news for us,' Jane said enthusiastically. Then she noticed Danny's expression. There was no doubt he didn't regard Harry's disclosure in a favourable light.

'If you're a *real* goalkeeper you don't want to play anywhere else,' Danny muttered, ignoring completely his own experience as an attacker and gleeful goalscorer.

'Only trying to help,' Harry said with a

shrug. 'That's why I spoke up. I mean, you guys have got Championship medals and I haven't. And I want to win one with the Kings.'

'Good point to end on,' Jane cut in briskly. 'Look, boys, there's nothing to be gained by going over the same ground again. You're probably all still hot and sweaty and need a shower to freshen up. So I'll leave you on your own. I'm sure it's been a good thing to try and work out where we went wrong. Now we've got to make sure we get everything *right* when we play Greendown. As Kieren said, all we have to do is forget the three points we didn't get and *collect* three points next time. See you for training on Tuesday.'

At the door she turned and looked back at them. Some were now standing up and about to get changed but almost without exception they were glum. 'Cheer up, boys!' she smiled. 'Remember, things can only get better.'

6 Crisis Moves

Things didn't get better. They got worse. After five matches Rodale Goal Kings, champions of the Highlea Sunday League, had only two points and were next to bottom of the League table. Played 5, won 0, drawn 2, lost 3, goals for 6, goals against 13. It was the stuff of nightmares and no one could predict when they would wake up.

Greendown, the second team to beat them, had played some inspired football. As with Torridon, that inspiration had probably come from the fact that they were competing against the champions. They wanted to prove they were as good as the best – or, at least, the best of the previous season. They wanted to dethrone the Kings and put themselves up as genuine contenders for the title. Sean Ferriby, Rodale's recruit from Greendown, had told Jane Allenby all he knew about his former team-mates; but he hadn't managed to guess at their improvement since he was in their ranks. They'd signed a particularly gifted midfielder who took control of events almost from the first kick, spraying the ball to all parts of the pitch with practically unerring accuracy to set up attacks or break up forays by the Kings. Jane tried to stifle his influence by putting Lloyd Colmer on to him as man-to-man marker; but that didn't work because the tall, strongly built Greendowner simply shrugged him off or, depressingly, outwitted him by clever footwork and body turns. It was he, of course, who set up the two goals by which Greendown won the match on their own lawn-smooth pitch on another sultry day.

Probably too late to make any difference, Jane had replaced Lloyd with Harry Greenland, hoping that his height might be effective in a close-marking role; and Sean had gone on as substitute for Frazer, who was perhaps still feeling the effects of his injury against Torridon. However, that tactic didn't work, either; as usual when someone was playing against his old team, Sean was given a particularly rough time, with every challenge resembling the outbreak of a minor war. Sean escaped without real injury but his legs were a mass of bruises. His coach feared he might suffer lasting psychological damage for he was unable to contribute anything at all to the Kings' cause.

On the surface there was some improvement in their next two games, both of them being drawn. Yet both were against opponents they traditionally beat comfortably and had expected to again, since neither Friday Bridge nor Bankhouse Invaders had started the season in notable form. All had gone according to plan against the Bridge with the Kings two up in the first twenty minutes, both scored by Davey although the second was just a tap-in after a Larry Hill shot was blocked on the line. Then Danny made a couple of mistakes that one spectator called 'howlers', and Jane couldn't disagree. Another missed punch led to the Bridge's first goal and their equalizer arrived when the Kings' keeper allowed a shot to bounce out of his arms and then bizarrely spin into the net off the back of his head. Late in the game Josh scored with a low-level header from a free kick only for

Friday Bridge to snatch a point with a solo goal practically on the stroke of full-time. To lose the lead once was bad enough, but to lose it twice was unforgivable; and Jane was unforgiving.

For the game with Bankhouse Invaders she made changes, dropping two of her regular defenders, Matthew Forest and Joe Parbold, normally a rock to rely on in all circumstances but strangely hesitant this season. She even wondered about replacing Dominic for he, too, was having a poor spell. She wouldn't have been surprised if any supporters had come up to her to suggest it but, thankfully, none had. Dominic himself remained tight-lipped at home about team matters and Jane didn't want to change her pattern of being his mum at home and his coach on the pitch.

Gareth Kingstree had been more successful in his new role than Harry Greenland, his partner in the centre of defence. She had fewer options in attack because the squad was short of strikers, as she now realized. Switching Reuben Jones and Larry Hill didn't quite work, although it was Reuben who scored after Bankhouse took the lead midway through the first half with an unstoppable half-volley from the edge of the penalty area. So that second successive draw hinted at a change of fortune for the Kings. Although they still hadn't won a game they'd at least been undefeated in the last two. So should she keep the same formation for the next match against Redville Rangers, Jane pondered. She still had faith in her players and they kept promising that they'd definitely win the next game. Well, most of them did: but, worryingly, one or two gave her the impression that they were resigned to defeat, that the Kings had no hope at all of holding on to their title. Danny Loxham, her skipper, was one of them.

Rather like Torridon, Redville were a strong, hard-running side and they quickly ran the Kings off their feet. By half-time they were three goals up and Jane was questioning the fitness of her boys. Had she trained them in the wrong way? Were her methods out of date and, in a word, hopeless? Nobody among the small crowd on yet another sweltering day was talking to her and there was no one with whom she could discuss the problems confronting her. None of the goals had been scored as a direct result of carelessness on the part of any defender. True, Harry was still too easily turned and his heading was, to say the least, weak. Danny, however, was actually in good form and but for him the score might well have been half-a-dozen by the interval. The one major fault she could identify was the half-heartedness of so many of the Kings. They just weren't battling hard enough for the ball.

'You've got to go out there and play as if your lives depended on it,' she told them as forcefully as possible. 'If you concede another three goals in the second half then you'd better look for another coach. I mean it!'

That was a gamble because she no longer had any idea whether they still wanted to play for her. She feared she might have lost their respect for her completely. These days they seemed far too introspective; the old bubbly spirit, their exuberance after scoring a goal, was missing. If things didn't improve very soon they'd cease to be a team she could recognize as her own.

Fortunately, some of their old determination and flair remained. Three minutes into the second half Reuben exchanged swift one-twos with Davey and then went on a scintillating solo run that took him round two defenders and the goalkeeper before he slid the ball into the net. A minute later he very nearly did it again but the goalie got a fingertip to his shot and turned the ball round the post for a corner. Five minutes after that Reuben went under to a scything tackle. He told Jane he wasn't really hurt but he was wincing for the rest of the game and never again made a worthwhile contribution. The Kings' revival was over and six minutes from time Redville made it 4–1 when Dominic tripped an opponent in the penalty area and the same player coolly converted the penalty kick.

It was just about the worst defeat Rodale Kings had suffered in a very long time. Jane was in despair. She knew she'd have to hold a crisis meeting with the entire squad to try to sort out their problems. But before that she needed to confide in someone, air her views and ideas and see whether they made sense to another person. Sam Saxton crossed her mind, but she wasn't sure that he really approved of the idea of the Kings having a female coach. Of course, he'd never hinted at anything like that but she suspected he was very old-fashioned at heart and hadn't caught up with changing fashions that affected football as much as any other sport or recreation these days. Part of her was tempted to seek advice from Dominic and invite him to speak openly about the team. After all, he had expressed an opinion (a little unexpectedly) during the changing-room inquest after the Torridon defeat. But no, it wouldn't be fair on him, Jane decided eventually. She knew he sometimes found it awkward to be the coach's son during a match or training. He really shouldn't be interrogated about his team-mates. Moreover, she had to admit, Dominic himself wasn't playing well this season. If she concluded that there'd have to be wholesale changes then Dominic could very well be one of them.

There was only one person she could consult and be sure of getting an honest opinion from in every respect: her husband,

Ken. They'd always had the best of relationships and Ken was happy to support her in whatever she attempted. On the other hand, he simply wasn't interested in soccer. He didn't attend Rodale's games because he was superstitious: he thought that if he were present they'd lose! Well, he hadn't attended one game yet this season and the Kings had still managed to lose three times. So that superstition, in Jane's eyes, was meaningless.

'Ken, I've simply got to talk to you about the Kings and all our troubles at present,' she began one evening as he was relaxing in front of the TV after a long day's work as a delivery driver. 'D'you mind? I mean, I basically want to bounce ideas off you, see what a practical person like you makes of them.'

'Fire away,' he invited. 'Just as long as there's nothing too technical like how to deal with overlapping wing-backs or forays down inside-right channels. That's the sort of jargon I think I hear when Dominic's watching the box. I can't make head nor tail of it!'

'No, it's nothing like that,' she laughed, although she was feeling far from cheerful. 'It's more about personalities and leadership and, well, overall strategy. You know what's been happening to us because you've kindly listened to my moans about all the points we've failed to pick up. Anyway, I think I've got to start trying to put things right by changing the captain. We need fresh leadership, some inspiration on the pitch. For some reason I can't fathom, Danny seems to have gone into his shell. And his form as a player is poor. He's making elementary mistakes, wants to punch the ball all the time instead of catch it, that sort of thing. Oh, and it's pretty obvious he and Harry Greenland don't hit it off.'

'Has he got over that rib injury, bruising you said it was?' Ken inquired. 'That might still be bothering him but he won't admit it.'

'You see, I *knew* you listened and took it all in when I told you my woes!' she said excitedly. 'I'm sure you've hit the nail on the head, Ken, because Danny is proud at heart and he'd never admit to anything being wrong if he could help it. I've asked him about that several times but he denies there's a problem. But, as I say, he's not a leader any longer so I'm going to replace him – *and* give him a complete break by putting someone else in goal.'

Ken's eyebrows rose. 'But I thought you didn't have another experienced goalkeeper? You said you were short of two vital players, another goalie and another striker.'

'Right again! But I think I may have solved the keeper worry. You see, Harry Greenland mentioned a little while ago that he used to play in goal. When I tackled him about it he admitted he quite liked that role. So I persuaded Davey to help me test him out – in secret, of course. Davey's very loyal to me: he wouldn't let on what's happening. Anyway, we had this practice session and Harry performed really well. So I'm going to give him his chance against Scorton. It's the biggest match of the season but I'm confident he's up to it. Oh, and Davey agrees with me.'

'Sounds a very positive move, then,' nodded her husband. 'But you really didn't need my help with that, did you?'

'Ah, but I do want to know what you think about the captaincy. Do you think I'd be overdoing it if I not only dropped Danny to the subs' bench but also stripped him of the captaincy? Not just for the Scorton match – I know he can't be skipper if he's not on the pitch – but in the long term?'

Ken Allenby didn't answer immediately. 'It's going to be a real sickener for him, losing out twice,' he said eventually. 'But from the little bit I know about Danny, well, I'm sure he'll bounce back. So yes, it might be all for the good in the long term.'

Jane nodded. 'Good. I'm sure Danny will cope. He's certainly coped with his mum's walk out. He and his dad have a great relationship. Oh, and he has his boxing to keep him going as well. *And* a girlfriend, I gather!'

'So the big question is, then, who're you going to award the captaincy to? Dominic?'

His wife pursed her lips. 'Do you think that could possibly be a good idea?' she asked in turn, giving the firm impression that she didn't think so.

'Up to you, darling. But I think Dom would quite like to be the boss on the pitch. He enjoys getting his own way, doesn't he?'

'I agree, but I just think he wouldn't want

to captain the Kings. He's been really good about keeping his distance from me where team matters are concerned. And I think the other players recognize that he won't carry tales from the changing room to me. They know I don't ask him anything that could be, well, personal about his team-mates. But if I suddenly promoted him to captain then I'm afraid they'd think my policy had changed, that I was putting my own son ahead of any of them.'

'Fair enough. You know best in that department. So who will you give the armband to? Little Davey?'

'Never let him hear you say that! Davey's very self-conscious about his height, or lack of it, rather. Not that it prevents him being brilliant in every way and he can certainly jump for a high ball. But no, I don't want anything to distract him from the job of scoring goals. And we're not getting enough of them at present. Oh, and I also prefer someone at the back, someone who can see it all happening in front of him.'

'Well then, who's that tall lad with the fair hair – had an eyesight problem at one time but overcame it. Very reliable, I think you said of him. And, yes, his mum is the one who always helps out, isn't she, even doing the team's laundry?'

'That's Karen Rowley. If you can remember all that, Ken, why can't you remember names? No, don't tell me! But Josh, well, he is very reliable and I'm sure he'd love to be captain. He's a bit injury-prone, though. Been all right so far this season, in spite of tumbles on rock-hard pitches, so maybe he's getting stronger. Still, I think he's not quite good enough as a player to be captain. The team like him well enough but I can't believe they *admire* his skills. And the skipper needs to command respect, don't you agree?'

'I expect so. Well, I don't think I can guess any more, so you'd better tell me. Oh, unless it's that lad with the terrifically loud voice – *Foggy*, that's the name. See, I do remember some!'

She laughed again. 'Unforgettable, he is! Thankfully, though, he's no longer in our squad. Walked out on us last season and hasn't been seen since. Well, not *in* a team, merely supporting one, Torridon. Turned up to shout for them just because they were playing us. He also took the opportunity to support Alex Todd, our other ex-King who was a bit of a trouble-maker. If Foggy *had* been on our books he'd've been badgering me like mad to make him the captain. It was what he always wanted. I have to admit, in some ways he might even have been good at the job. Against that, though, most of the other players couldn't stand his boasting and non-stop noise. Always had to be the centre of attention.'

Ken sighed theatrically. 'Well, I'm sure I'll never guess who you *have* chosen, so you'd better tell me. I don't want to break things off but I do have some paperwork to finish this evening.'

'Darling, I am sorry: didn't mean to go on and on. But it's just so helpful to be able to think aloud like this. Honestly, it really focuses my mind. Anyway, I've decided that Kieren Kelly should be captain. He's –'

'– the boy with the mum who's an attractive blonde who used to be a singer and had a French boyfriend who sent his son over to play for the Kings when you won the Cup!'

Ken cut in triumphantly to show that he was still concentrating.

'*Very* good!' she applauded. 'Except that Karl-Heinz's father is German. He simply lived in France because he had a restaurant there. Anyway, you're right. I've gone for Kieren because he's having easily his best season – and he was pretty good *last* season. He suddenly gained confidence and started to express himself. In spite of those stick-thin legs he has terrific speed. I'm sure the rest of the squad respect his skills and his ability to win the ball and set up openings. So I honestly think it's worth trying him out as captain. He'll lead us from the front – even if he does officially play at the back!'

'Well, things really *must* be improving if you can crack a joke about the Kings!' Ken grinned. 'I was beginning to think you and your team had descended into a state of permanent gloom.'

'Oh no, there's always some light at the end of the tunnel. I've just had my eyes closed to it, that's all. Ken, you've been a marvel. You've helped much more than you'd imagine. Now I really feel I know what I'm doing – and I'm going to do it now. No time like the present. I'll give Kieren a ring and see how he reacts to the idea of taking over from Danny. I mean, if he turns it down there's no point in telling Danny I've had to make that particular change.'

It was Jakki who answered the phone and she launched into her own speech before Jane could even mention Kieren. 'Oh, Jane, I'm so glad you've rung because I was about to call you. I think it would be a good idea if you and I had a down-to-earth chat. I mean, *something's* got to be done about our team before we sink without trace. We can't possibly go on like we have been doing, can we? One or two mums have had a word with me. I can tell you they've got a lot of questions to ask about what's going wrong. I can't blame –'

'Oh, but nobody's said anything to me,' Jane cut in, not entirely truthfully. Serena Colmer, Lloyd's mum and a most enthusiastic Kings supporter, had mentioned at the Redville match that it didn't look as though a second successive championship was on the cards.

'Only a matter of time, Jane, I'm sure of that,' Jakki continued. 'I expect they're hoping I'll take the initiative and try to sort something out. I mean, they know how keen I am on everything to do with football: tactics, training, team selection, oh, the lot, really.'

Jane didn't have any doubt what she was hearing: Jakki was making it plain that she was ready to step into Jane's shoes as the Kings' coach if a vacancy arose or could be created. In the past, Jakki had more than once hinted that she'd be pleased to act as Jane's assistant if invited; but Jane wasn't sure that Kieren's mum really knew enough about the game to do that job. It had always seemed to her that Jakki's chief ambition was to promote Kieren's cause as a footballer. Maybe, though, she had misjudged the former pop singer.

'Jakki, I can promise you I've been doing very little else but thinking hard about what needs to be done to improve our results. I even wake up in the middle of the night worrying about the Kings! So – no, hang on a minute, let me finish – I definitely know action has to be taken. And I've taken it. That's why I'm ringing you. Actually, it was

Kieren I was wanting a word with. Is he there?'

'Oh yes, he is, but just on his way out, as it happens. Kieren! Mrs Allenby wants a word with you. When you've finished don't ring off. I'm in the middle of a conversation. Here he is, Jane.'

Jane could sense from the way he answered that he was expecting bad rather than good news. Perhaps that was unavoidable in the light of what had been happening to his team. So when he was asked how he'd feel about taking over as skipper he wasn't sure what to say.

'Kieren, I really do want you to lead the squad,' Jane added to help him along. 'I'm sure your influence will be vital in getting us out of this bad run. You're such a positive player and that's bound to rub off on the other boys.'

In the moments before he answered she wondered what she'd do if he turned her down. It would have to be Davey, she supposed.

'OK, Coach, I'll do it,' he announced. 'And thanks for asking me. Just hope Danny's not going to be mad at me.'

'Danny'll be fine,' she tried to reassure him. 'He's not the selfish type. Like you, he's a team player. I'm going to see him presently and I'll tell him what you've said. Your mum said you were going out so I'll let you go, Kieren. See you at training on Tuesday.'

After a longer-than-hoped-for chat with Jakki, who clearly was delighted by Kieren's new role as captain of the Kings, she tried to reach Danny. But Danny, his dad reported, had gone out to see a friend, though which friend that was Mr Loxham didn't know. Ah well, said Jane, it wasn't essential to talk to him now. She promised to ring again next day.

Originally, Danny had set out to visit Karl, a schoolmate he did some sparring with at intervals. They had the same boxing coach and he wanted to know whether Karl, too, felt that Hurricane Hogan wasn't doing enough to find them quality opponents. If they were going to reach the top then they needed to be tested by equally ambitious fighters. Unfortunately, however, Karl had gone fishing. *Fishing*! Danny couldn't believe that anyone, let alone a boxer, could waste time on such a boring, passive pastime.

Now, Danny decided, he'd wasted enough time trying to find Karl; instead, he'd go and see Andrea. Once he'd made that decision, however, he moved cautiously. Even if she was at home she might not want to see him. He'd tried to talk to her several times since the Torridon match when she'd criticized his performance but they'd never managed anything that could be called a conversation. When he'd phoned there'd been 'urgent' reasons why she couldn't talk for long; and when he saw her at the Bankhouse game he couldn't detach her from the girl she was arm-in-arm with, another tallish blonde but nowhere near as attractive as Andrea in Danny's eyes. He simply didn't know where he stood with her and it was time to find out; on the other hand, he worried about receiving an outright rejection if he did manage to see her. Hence the slow journey to her home on the other side of Rodale.

By the time he reached the McKinnon house it was practically dark but lights were shining out so at least someone was at home. Danny's first worry was that Oats would answer the door and thus he'd have to ask him to fetch Andrea – and that would give her the chance to say she wasn't in if she didn't want to see him. Maybe, it occurred to him, she was in the back garden, which was large enough to contain the grassed area where, they'd told him, Oats and Andrea practised their soccer skills together, *and* a barbecue pit *and* a white-painted summer-house. Hoping no one was watching him he strolled round to the back of the house and let himself into the garden. His heart sank. No one to be seen. Unless, of course, they were in the summer-house which faced the back of the house. Without thinking about aspects of trespassing he flitted across the lawn and approached it from the rear. As he carefully made his way round to the railed verandah he thought he heard a voice, a kind of stifled laugh. But then all was quiet again.

It was barely light enough to see the interior so he climbed the couple of steps and peered in. Then, as his eyes became accustomed to the gloom, he could see Andrea – and the boy who was with her. As she shouted 'What are you doing here, Danny?' they sprang apart and there was some hasty adjusting of clothing, although as far as he could see they were both wearing only shorts and T-shirts.

'Er, I was just well, wanting to see you – you know, see you,' he stammered. 'I didn't know you were in here,' he added, realizing how foolish he sounded.

'I was just talking privately with Kieren,' Andrea said, resuming a normal voice and standing up.

'Hi, Danny,' said Kieren, who was still sitting, slightly hunched, on the twin seat they had been occupying. Danny couldn't tell whether he was embarrassed or not at being discovered.

For a moment no one seemed to know what to say or do next. Danny supposed he should walk away but he'd never felt so attracted to Andrea. In the half-light she looked even lovelier than usual.

Then, feeling he had to say something to his team-mate, Kieren murmured sympathetically: 'Sorry about the captaincy, Danny mate. I didn't ask for it, you know. I was just given it.'

'The *captaincy*? What're you on about?' Danny demanded.

'Oh!' Kieren knew at once he'd made a terrible blunder. It was bad enough Danny having to find him with the girl Danny himself fancied; but now he'd given him news he must hate. 'Sorry, but I thought Jane would've told you by now. She said she was going to.'

'Tell me *what*?' Danny persisted, although by now he'd guessed what was coming.

Kieren swallowed hard, wishing like mad that Danny would just go away so that he could resume his loving relationship with Andrea. 'Well, Jane has decided that the Kings ought to have a change of skipper. She thinks that we ought to, well, do better than we are doing and she asked me to take on the job. I said yes. I mean, if you aren't the captain then I think I'm the best player for the job. Danny, I'm really sorry to break it to you. Honestly, I thought you *must* know by now.'

'Well, I didn't. Thanks for nothing, Kieren.' Danny turned away, jumped down the steps to the lawn and then walked away as calmly as he could manage. Already he was working out that if he'd been stripped of the captaincy then he'd probably lost his place in the team as well. He knew he'd been in poor form and Mrs Allenby had to do something to get the team back on a winning track. Only problem was, who could she possibly put in goal? Gareth Kingstree was really the only possibility, but Danny knew that Gareth didn't like keeping goal.

Still, it wasn't his problem, was it? He didn't want to think about it. It had been a terrible evening for him. He'd suffered a hat-trick of disasters. At this moment, he couldn't say which was the worst of them.

'Oh dear,' was what Andrea said when he departed. 'I do feel sorry for him. That was an awful way for him to find out.'

Kieren sat up. 'You're not blaming me, are you?'

'No, of course not. You weren't to know he was going to creep up on us like that. But he looked so *hurt*. Wish I could make it up to him somehow.'

Now Kieren was alarmed. 'But you won't, will you? You won't give up on me, will you?'

'Course not!' she grinned and went to sit

beside him again. 'How could I when we've only just started?'

When the news reached Davey Stroud, via a phone call from Larry Hill, his first reaction was one of disappointment that *he* hadn't been made captain. After all, he was the star striker, the player whose goals had helped to bring them the Championship, the Player of the Season. Davey guessed that he was probably the coach's favourite player and so it would have been completely understandable if he'd been awarded the role. Still, he couldn't really complain. At least he was virtually a fixture in the side, so Mrs Allenby could have no reason to drop him. Which was more than could be said for Larry. His worries about his place were the real reason he'd rung Davey, trying to check whether his co-striker knew more than he did about the choice of team for the match with Scorton Aces.

'I haven't a clue, Larry,' Davey said. 'I know everybody thinks the coach must tell me secrets because she picked me as her top player, but I swear she doesn't. Fact is, I think she bends over backwards *not* to have favourite players. Even Dom couldn't tell you who she likes best. *I* thought it was Danny but, well, she's sacked him now, hasn't she, so it can't be him. Tell you what, why don't you ring her and ask her if you're in the team? Then you can quit worrying.'

'Oh, I couldn't do that, Davey,' his co-striker replied hurriedly. 'That's like *asking* to be selected, isn't it? No coach would go for that. Probably drop you for – what's the word? – yeah, impertinence!'

'Don't think she'd react like that, Larry,' Davey laughed. 'But please yourself.'

Larry hadn't been taking his chances on the pitch; and now he wasn't going to take any risks with his future.

One player who didn't hesitate to contact his coach when he felt it might be to his advantage to phone her was Josh Rowley. Annoyingly, he had to wait until both his mum and his sister Chrissie had completed *their* telephone conversations before he could ring her.

'Why don't you go round and *see* your boyfriend instead of phoning him up all the time?' he inquired mildly as at last he picked up the receiver.

Chrissie gave him a withering look. 'You simply wouldn't understand. You know nothing about girls.'

He had no answer to that but thankfully it was Jane, not Dominic, who answered.

'Oh, Josh, how nice to hear from you,' was her encouraging greeting. By now her normal cheerfulness had returned as a result of taking firm decisions about the composition of the Kings' next team. Then, remembering how injury-prone Josh was inclined to be, she added: 'You're all right, aren't you? Haven't hurt yourself or anything?'

The question rather surprised him but he managed to laugh it off. 'No, no, I'm fine, honestly. Can I ask you something very personal?'

'Well, of course you can,' Jane replied without hesitation, in spite of wondering what on earth he had in mind.

'Can I play as a striker against Scorton? In place of Larry, I mean. I'm not trying to stab Larry in the back or anything like that but he just isn't getting any goals, is he? And, Mrs

Allenby, I do score goals. You've seen that. I *used* to play as a striker before Mr Todd made me play at the back. I know I can do it, honestly. Davey Stroud and I would be a great partnership.'

Because he'd said so much Jane had time to prepare a reply. For once her decision wasn't going to hurt anyone (well, not immediately: Larry could be told later). 'Josh I'm so pleased you have asked because that means you *really* want to play up front. I wasn't absolutely sure of that. But, anyway, the answer is yes.'

He could hardly believe it. He'd been so sure she'd turn the idea down that he'd prepared a list of reasons why he felt she should change her mind; now he instinctively screwed up that scrap of paper and tossed it towards the wastepaper basket on the other side of the room. It went in.

'That's great!' he enthused. 'Mrs Allenby, I know I'll do well. Davey and I are good mates, really. I know how he likes to receive the ball. So I'll be delivering loads of good passes as well as banging in the goals myself.'

'That's what I want to hear, Josh,' she told him warmly. 'You've been invaluable at the back and you deserve to show what you can do up front. But don't say anything to Larry about this. I must tell him myself. He's only dropping to the subs' bench, so his chance will come again. I'm having to do a reshuffle in defence but I have high hopes it'll all work out. Anyway, Josh, we'll talk about things in detail at our training session. We've got to get out of this bad run. So I hope your goals will do the trick.'

'Oh, they will, Coach, I promise you that,' Josh replied fervently.

The last phone call of the evening was also to the Allenby household, but this time it was for Dominic. His father answered, thought he recognized the distinctive voice but didn't question it when the caller described himself as 'a friend'.

'Who is it?' asked a mystified Dominic when he picked up the receiver.

'Marc – Marc Thrale,' said the familiar voice.

'Oh, Foggy. What –'

'Just keep your voice down!' insisted Foggy, obviously unaware of the irony of that request. 'Don't want your mum to know who's calling. I'd've rung off if she'd answered. Listen, can you get away after the match against us next Sunday? There's –'

'*Us*? Who's us? Oh, are you playing for Scorton now?'

'Course I am! Don't you know anything about the rest of the Highlea Sunday League? Anyway, this is nothing to do with the Aces or the Kings. It's the future I'm talking about, Dom. *Your* future. You want to go to the top, don't you?'

Dominic had no problem with that question. 'Of course.'

'Right, then, I've got something to show you, something you won't want to miss. Kieren has already signed up so –'

'Kieren? *Our* Kieren? But he's playing for us. He can't sign for anyone else. That's crazy!'

'*Signed up* – I'm just talking metaphorically. Isn't that what they call it? Dom, I'm talking about the future. Your future as well as Kieren's. The *future* is what's important. So think about it. And I'll talk to you on Sunday. But don't tell anyone else about this phone call. OK?'

And the phone went dead before Dominic could formulate any kind of reply.

7 *The Way Back*

Jane Allenby wasn't the only one who felt that anything that could be changed about the Kings had changed since their last match, the defeat by Redville. Even the weather was different, the long hot spell having given way to cool, rainy days. Jakki Kelly, turning up in a spectacular red-and-yellow waterproof, was also wearing her brightest smile.

'Feels like a whole new beginning, doesn't it, Jane?' she remarked. 'I'm sure our fortunes are about to improve. Kieren has promised me they will. I can tell you, he's really excited about being the captain. You won't regret that move, Jane.'

The coach was pleased, if a little surprised, by the support her changes had brought, even before they were tested in the home game with Scorton Aces, the current League leaders. She'd expected the squad meeting before the previous Tuesday's training session to be a tense, possibly even acrimonious, affair. It had been nothing of the sort. Even Danny had said very little (but then she'd had a long talk with him earlier to emphasize that he wasn't being discarded, merely rested for a while, and that it was up to him to fight for his place as first-choice goalkeeper again. He'd said he would.) Larry had grumbled a bit, but that just reflected his father's customary attitude when things weren't perfect; what appeared to upset him most was that he was being replaced by someone he regarded as 'just an ordinary defender'.

Josh, of course, was bubbling with enthusiasm. Jane noticed that Karen, his mum, was also in a relaxed mood, probably partly, at least, because Josh was less likely to injure himself on a rain-soaked surface. In fact, he had been completely free of injuries of any sort for a long time now and Jane supposed he was stronger altogether since he'd stopped growing so quickly. He was in animated conversation with Davey, doubtless plotting their combined moves designed to unlock Scorton's steely defence. To her surprise,

Davey had arrived with a girl; she had short, dark hair and, almost inevitably, she was a little taller than him. They appeared to be on good terms already and Jane wondered how long it might be before Dominic acquired a girlfriend (unless, secretly, he already had). She knew that Danny was dating someone because he'd once triumphantly mentioned it to her, so probably some of the others were, too. So far, though, whatever romances existed among her squad none had been a problem when it came to training and playing.

Because he'd had to take one of his siblings to a birthday party early that evening Reuben Jones had missed the training session, so Jane now made a point of filling him in on what had happened and why she'd made changes. It was part of her philosophy that squad members were entitled to know why she did what she did, for then no one could complain he didn't know what was expected of him or his team-mates. Some coaches, she knew, just issued orders to their players and explained nothing (so, often, they were the ones who yelled loudest and longest during matches).

Now she reminded Reuben that she wanted him to support their strikers and, she added, he was to forge links with Lloyd Colmer, who from now on would operate in a more central midfield position.

'I think you made a good choice in Kieren as captain, Boss,' he confided to her. 'Don't get me wrong. I've nothing against Danny. I like him. But Kieren is our best player and he always knows who to pass to. Danny had sort of lost some confidence, hadn't he?'

Jane nodded, greatly impressed by her playmaker's insight and his assessment of Kieren. Even as he led his team out he was fingering the armband, plainly proud to be wearing it. Automatically, she looked for Foggy in the opposition's navy-and-old-gold shirts and navy shorts. Predictably, he was running out alongside their skipper, clapping loudly and calling: 'Come on the Aces, let's get stuck into 'em!'

Dominic had warned her that his old team-mate would be playing for Scorton. She was grateful he hadn't kept the information to himself, although he hadn't mentioned where he'd got it from and she hadn't asked. After thinking about it, she'd decided there was nothing to be gained from making any plan to deal with him. Foggy would still presumably be the old Foggy, full of energy and enthusiasm and with occasional flashes of inspired play but all too ready to retreat into anonymity if things didn't go absolutely right for him. She simply warned her players that they should be prepared for Foggy's over-physical tackles. She wouldn't have been surprised if someone like Kieren had said 'We'll deal with *him*', but nobody had.

Scorton had a good following and, to Jane's relief, there was a fair crowd of home supporters. Jane still worried privately that her predecessor as coach (or, indeed, someone else like Jakki or her husband, Clark) would seek an opportunity to prise her job away from her.

The Kings kicked off with the rain blowing into their faces and within moments the new strike force proved it might become very profitable. His confidence high, Josh displayed very deft footwork in rounding two opponents before sliding the perfect pass for Davey to run on to. Davey's alertness and electric pace did the rest as he reached the ball almost before Scorton's central defenders had realized the danger to them. With a clever spin and then a sideways jink Davey completely changed the direction of attack before feeding Reuben on the right flank. Inevitably, Lefty spun too in order to deliver a cross from his favoure foot. It was all Josh could have wished for and the only fault lay with him: his powered header was a fraction too high. The ball hit the bar instead of the net. Scorton's goalie was taking no chances with the rebound and flapped it over the bar to concede a corner.

'Brilliant start, Kings!' Jane yelled delightedly.

The applause all around her showed that the home fans were thankful to see their much-criticized team starting so well. A goal now would be a wonderful bonus. Unfortunately, that wasn't the Kings' reward. This time an equally tall defender beat Josh to the ball and when Reuben gained possession his shot was easily collected by the keeper.

For several minutes the Kings managed to maintain that level of pressure. Yet they couldn't get the ball into the net. Davey came closest with a left-foot drive on the turn from another Josh pass; the Aces' keeper only just got his fingers to the ball to push it round the post. Once again, Scorton's chimney-tall defenders cleared the danger from the resultant corner.

With Foggy dropping deeper and deeper in order to get into the game the Aces' attack wasn't functioning at all. Jane relayed a message to Kieren to move up with Frazer when Rodale won free kicks or corners; for some reason they seemed reluctant to advance beyond their own penalty area at those times.

But perhaps they'd made the right decision, Jane mentally acknowledged a couple of minutes later. For the siege of Scorton's goalmouth was suddenly relieved when their keeper threw the ball out to Foggy. And Foggy, eager to make his mark on the game, kept possession and accelerated. He kept going at the same pace, passed to his co-striker, demanded the return, swept past Joe Parbold with a clever dip of the shoulder and lined up a shot. Harry had come off his line and plainly wasn't clear what to do. Before he made up his mind Foggy hit a thunderbolt.

The ball rocketed past the keeper, struck the inside of the left-hand post and then ricocheted across the goalmouth. Harry had no chance whatsoever of reaching it but Kieren, racing back like a greyhound, managed to get to it ahead of Scorton's other striker. And, calmly, Kieren took possession, turned with the ball and then delivered a long, accurate pass to Reuben. Danger over – for the moment.

'How unlucky can you get?' Foggy roared, his hands to his head, knees buckling, in real and theatrical despair. Nobody, really, could disagree with that view. None the less, there were some jeers from Rodale supporters and cries of 'Go home, Foggy, you're a traitor!'

Jane raised her eyebrows but didn't say anything. It was one of her chief worries that, like Alex Todd, Marc Thrale would be inspired by playing against his old team and score a thoroughly damaging goal. It was the perfect revenge, in their eyes. All she could hope now was that Marc would become increasingly desperate through failing to get that desired goal. Then his overall play would suffer.

Her main worry concerned Harry Greenland: would he really be able to keep goal successfully in a competitive match? After all, it was a long time since he'd had that role and, of course, it hadn't been at this level of play. In her mind, choosing him was the only real gamble of all her changes for this match. He was untested and the way he'd reacted to Foggy's raid didn't fill her with confidence that she'd done the right thing. He hadn't panicked; but equally he hadn't looked secure.

'He'll be all right. We've all got to learn, you know,' said Danny, who was now standing beside her, wearing his track suit over his football kit.

'That's generous of you, Danny, and just like you,' she smiled. All the same, she was astonished he could be so philosophical after being deprived of the captaincy as well as his place in the team for today.

Danny just nodded at that compliment. He'd done a lot of thinking since discovering Kieren with Andrea. He didn't blame his team-mate because he had no doubt Andrea was the treacherous one; she'd let him down just as Sophie had. Well, one of these days he'd find a girl who genuinely liked him. Then they'd never split. Meanwhile, he was going to concentrate on his boxing and football. He had no doubts whatsoever that he had a talent for both sports. Soon, he'd win his place back in goal for the Kings. Harry, he was sure, wouldn't keep him out.

And, just as he was reflecting on that, Harry showed he couldn't keep the Aces out. To his almost unstoppable joy, the goal was fashioned by Foggy. Picking up a loose ball after a midfield mêlée he set off on one of his barnstorming runs through the middle. Kieren's sliding tackle was a microsecond too late to win the ball and when Foggy swerved past Joe he had a clear sight of goal. Naturally, he unleashed a ferocious shot. Harry, off his line, found it coming straight at him but couldn't hold it. The ball bounced back off his chest and Scorton's alert top goal-scorer, Charlie Portland, racing in at speed, picked up the rebound and neatly slid it past the stranded keeper into the net. He and Foggy danced back to the middle like dervishes.

'Typical Foggy luck!' Danny snorted. 'But he'll claim he set up the greatest goal ever.'

Jane didn't think it mattered what Foggy said: the only important thing was that the Kings were a goal down after dominating the game. Was their season never going to improve? She didn't think she could blame Harry because at least he'd got in the way of the shot. 'Come on, Kings, don't let your heads drop!' she yelled. Most of the rest of the home fans, she realized, were saying nothing. Many of them were already suspecting that the champions were about to lose again.

Two minutes later, they were sure of it. Once again the irrepressible Foggy provided the launching pad for the aerial raid on Rodale's defenders. This time he whipped a superb pass down the left flank to the goal-scorer and Charlie cut inside, had a tussle with Oats, emerged still in possession and then fed Foggy. Joe, determined not to be beaten a second time, stuck out a foot and diverted the ball over the line for a corner. It was the first of three because twice the ball was bundled to safety over the line to prevent

Scorton adding to their lead. But nothing could be done about the incident that followed the third kick.

Josh, defending keenly, headed the ball down into a thicket of hacking legs; and when the ball flew up again Oats instinctively flung out a hand to protect his face. The ref was probably the only person present who felt that *wasn't* an involuntary act. Whistle shrilling he pointed to the penalty spot.

'Never in this world!' Jane gasped, while Danny muttered something unprintable. And Jane was too incensed to reprimand him. She sympathized with the protests her players on the pitch were making to the ref, although she thought she'd drummed it into them that officials never changed their minds as a result of players' complaints or, worse, abuse. So she winced and thought about how she would deal with them later when both Oats and Josh received yellow cards for dissent.

No one remained calmer than Charlie Portland. Although Foggy pleaded with him to be allowed to take the penalty against a team he was so desperate to humiliate, Charlie was conceding nothing. He was the official penalty-taker and that was that. Then he showed how good he was at the task by sending Harry in the wrong direction and slotting the ball into the net by the right-hand post. Rodale Goal Kings 0 Scorton Aces 2.

'Didn't think our luck could get any worse,' murmured Jakki, coming to stand beside Jane and offer sympathy.

'Good penalty, though – unstoppable,' acknowledged Danny.

Jakki gave him a sharp glance as if questioning his loyalty now that he'd been deposed as skipper and keeper.

'Oh, Danny's always fair-minded, he knows how impossible those shots are to stop,' Jane explained, reading Jakki's mind. 'You know, Jakki, I can't believe I've made the wrong moves and *that's* why we're two goals down. But, well, it's not just bad luck, is it?'

'Jane, we're right behind you, all the Kings' real supporters are,' Jakki stressed. 'I know the boys believe in themselves. Kieren does. You all do, don't you, Danny?'

'*Definitely*! Nobody's letting us down. I mean, the Aces are a really good side, you know. Nearly beat us to the title last season and they look *stronger* this time.'

'You're making me feel a lot better, Danny,' his coach told him, and she meant every word.

All the same, at half-time the score was unchanged. None the less, Jane's only criticism concerned her players' protests to the ref. If they made any more then they'd suffer the consequences in not being picked to play in future matches. Harry apologized for failing to prevent both goals but Jane said she wasn't blaming him. She didn't want to undermine his confidence, although privately she'd decided that if he did make another real mistake then she might have to replace him with Danny. After all, Harry was still a useful outfield player.

'Josh, you're having a great game and you're helping the defence enormously,' she told the fair-haired all-rounder. 'But if we're going to get anything out of this game I need you up front with Davey. We've just got to get goals, OK?'

'Right!' he responded eagerly. He vowed to get one of those goals if it killed him.

By the start of the second half the rain was heavier and mistakes were being made all over the slippery pitch. The Kings' defence, however, appeared sure-footed and Harry's handling couldn't be faulted when he came out to take high crosses.

Kieren had noted that his mum was standing beside Jane Allenby and wondered what they were talking about. He'd already decided he ought to be more positive in all he was doing, so when Lloyd intercepted a misguided pass intended for Foggy Kieren sprinted forward and called for the ball. Willingly, Lloyd supplied it. Kieren's pace hadn't been demonstrated so far to the Scorton players and he was past three of them before they realized what he was up to on his diagonal run.

'Go on, Kieren, go for it!' Jakki yelled. Jane joined in: 'Yes, Kieren, keep going!'

Giving no sign that he'd heard them, the Kings' new skipper exchanged a one–two with Lefty, swerved, lost the ball, fought to regain it, looked up and then hit a left-foot drive towards the top of the net. Unfortunately for the Kings, the wind that had got up carried it just wide of the upright, with the Scorton goalkeeper open-mouthed in surprise at the closeness of that escape.

'Well done!' 'Great run!' 'Kings rule!' The chants of the home supporters were ringing out for the first time in ages. Jane was delighted to see that Danny, too, was on his feet yelling his support. She felt that had to mean that her former captain didn't have any animosity towards his successor.

Next time Kieren had the ball Scorton didn't back off: but, again, Kieren took players on and beat them. Until, that is, Foggy hurtled in like a runaway steer. The 'Ooooooh that went round the ground were as much for the force as the effect of it as Kieren went crashing down and rolled over and over. Jane was dashing to his rescue before the ref could even think of signalling for her; in any case, he was busy taking Marc Thrale's name and holding up a yellow card. It had, he told the offender, very nearly been a red card.

To her great relief Jane found that Kieren wasn't really damaged at all. His legs might be thin but they were whipcord strong. All the same, she took her time checking out any problems with probing fingers. It wasn't a bad thing for him to have a breather.

'Kieren, you're in inspired form, so keep it up as long as you can,' she told him. 'I don't think Marc will risk another tackle like that. The last thing he wants is to be sent off against us.'

'OK,' Kieren agreed. 'We can still win this, you know.'

The rest of the Kings seemed to think so, too. Frazer was the next defender to move forward menacingly. Again, uncertain what was coming, Scorton gave ground. This time it was a defender who gave away a free kick only a couple of metres outside the penalty area. As usual, Lefty was going to take it, for none of the Kings doubted his ability to put the ball just where he wanted it. Davey edged into the middle with Kieren alongside him before they started darting sideways and back again in a rehearsed routine to baffle their markers. Josh had drifted out to the left and no one followed him. But Lefty surprised them all by switching the ball to the right where Oats was loitering.

Oats knew exactly what was needed. Without doing more than steadying himself he drove the ball powerfully across the box towards Josh who was already moving in, still unmarked. Josh, too, had a plan. Fiercely he hammered the ball into the heart of the box at about knee-height. None of the Aces could control it. Then, when it bounced from the thigh of a central defender no more than a metre from the goal-line Davey hurled himself forward horizontally to head the ball into the net, which it reached after glancing off the helpless goalkeeper's hip.

It was a brave as well as a vital goal and the Kings' fans jumped up and down in their excitement as they applauded it. Davey had rolled over and out of danger from anyone after making contact with the ball only to be swamped by his team-mates. Jane winced: she was always worried that players would suffer a severe injury as a result of over-exuberant celebrations.

As she glanced along the touchline she saw that possibly no one was looking more pleased than the dark-haired girl she'd seen with Davey earlier, and who was now talking enthusiastically to a stocky woman with similar colouring who was almost certainly her mother. If they were going to become supporters then it might be a good idea to welcome them, Jane decided.

'Am I right in thinking you're Davey's girlfriend?' she inquired amiably as she came up to them.

The girl's eyes widened in surprise. 'No way!' she exploded.

The woman laughed. 'This is Katie and she's Davey's sister. And I'm his mum, Jenny Stroud,' she explained, smiling broadly. 'We promised we'd come and support him one day and today's the day. I think he must have scored that goal to impress us, and we're impressed, aren't we, Katie?'

'Oh, definitely!' was the response in a jokey kind of way, although Jane suspected she really meant it.

Then Danny wandered up to join them so Jane introduced him. Right away she could tell that he was interested in Katie. There was no doubt in Jane's mind that he had a way with girls, just as he related so easily to practically everyone he met. He was, she decided, a real asset to the Kings. He hadn't once moaned about his demotion and she was sure he'd fight his way back into the team.

They all exchanged a few more snippets of information before Jane murmured that she'd better concentrate on the game again. But she'd learned that Davey's dad was on 'walkabout' again, which explained his absence.

The goal had really fired up the champions and now Scorton were having to repel wave after wave of attacks. Only Foggy remained up front, prowling around the half-way line, desperate for any chance at all to get the goal he craved. His captain, though, wanted *everyone* back. Foggy's expression would have frightened a grizzly bear as he reluctantly obeyed the summons.

When, shortly afterwards, the former King scythed down Davey on the edge of the box Jane expected to see the red card. Foggy, though, was in luck: the indulgent ref simply gave him a final warning, probably because he didn't like sending a boy off. In any case, Foggy's vengeful tackle was to prove the undoing of his team.

Once again there was a flurry of activity as attackers and defenders moved this way and that as they tried to take up prime positions. No one was more agitated than the goalie, who'd been told by his coach that he was responsible for the Kings' goal. This time Josh moved to a central spot only a metre or so from the line.

Not knowing what to expect from this free kick the Aces were fractionally slow to rise when Reuben flashed the ball into the heart of their defence. That hardly mattered because Josh climbed higher than anyone, meeting the ball perfectly with his forehead to send it over the goalkeeper's stretching arms into the top of the net.

By any reckoning, it was a classic centre-forward's header from a set piece and Josh had good reason to turn handsprings, his new form of celebration. Jane was just as thrilled that her tactical change had worked, exactly as Josh had promised her it would.

'Kings are going top, Kings are going TOP!' someone sang out as a variation of the 'Kings Rule' chant. Not true by a long way: but Jakki, too, was gripped by the change in their fortunes.

'What a turnaround!' she exclaimed. 'Look

at Kieren, geeing everybody up. He's a real captain, isn't he, Jane?'

'Absolutely,' agreed the coach. She, like every other Rodale supporter, was anxiously looking at her watch to see how much time remained. Scorton had settled for a point: they weren't even interested in moving out of their own half, although occasionally they managed to hoof the ball to the half-way line for Foggy to chase. He'd spent the minimum amount of time in defence and all that interested him was getting a goal. He wasn't even thinking about whether it might be the winner for his team.

Twice within a minute the Kings had shots cleared off the line and once Davey was convinced he'd scored only for the ref to rule that Josh had been offside. It was the most marginal of decisions and Jane momentarily worried about her players' reactions. More yellow cards might lead to problems with suspensions later in the season. Kieren, though, was alert to that and hastily shoved team-mates away from any contact with the ref.

That was virtually the last kick of the game.

The rain had stopped and when the final whistle sounded the Kings had gained a point and the world looked a little brighter to their supporters who applauded them from the pitch. It was noticeable that Marc didn't shake hands with any of the Kings.

'But we can't congratulate ourselves,' Jane pointed out in the changing-room. 'We still haven't won a game this season. We're the champions, yet we're still near the bottom of the pile.'

'Not for long, Coach,' Kieren assured her. 'We *nearly* won today. That was against the best team we'll play this season. And I think we'll get stronger. Honestly, we played some good stuff today.'

The rest of the players either nodded or used some other phrase to agree with him. Danny went further: he clapped and said, 'Dead right, Skipper.' The diplomat was becoming silkier by the minute, Jane smiled to herself. Of Larry Hill, one of the other substitutes, there was no sign. Instead of joining everyone else in the changing-room he'd gone straight home.

Jane left them to get changed and have

showers but she took Davey's comment to Josh with her: 'Tell you one of the best things about this game: Foggy didn't score. He didn't put one over us, even though he tried to kick me out of the game with that killer tackle. I tell you, Josh, Foggy Thrale is history. The Kings are the future.'

Those almost poetic words of Davey's were what Jane remembered when, the following morning, she had a phone call from Jakki Kelly and heard the terrible news about Marc's accident.

'He was out on his bike on the village by-pass when this truck hit him,' Jakki reported. 'Don't know who is to blame but Liz – you know, a pal of mine who's a nurse – well she reckons Foggy just shot out of nowhere, going like a maniac across the dual carriageway. The trucker didn't stand a chance. He was so shocked he was kept in hospital overnight.'

'So, how bad is Foggy?' Jane asked.

'*Very* bad. Not life-threatening but, well, probably football-threatening. I mean, one leg is so badly broken it may take months to put right, if they can do it at all. At the moment they don't know the extent of his other injuries.'

'How awful! I must go and see him, Jakki. What about you?'

'Yes, of course. Kieren wants to go, too, but I think he should wait a bit. Perhaps go with a friend rather than with you or me. What d'you think?'

'I agree. I'm sure that's the best arrangement. Oh, poor Marc! What a terrible thing to happen to a boy who loves his football.'

8 Winning Again

As they approached Highlea General Hospital's main entrance both of them automatically slowed down. 'Don't really know why I'm here. I really hate hospitals,' Kieren murmured, glancing at the blue-and-white sign which listed all the various departments and their locations.

'Why's that?' Danny asked.

'I came to visit my dad when he was here for some stomach surgery – minor, that's what they said it was. But the smells and noises, people yelling out in pain, they were pretty terrible.'

'Oh, they're OK if you ignore the bits you don't like,' Danny responded. 'Boxers have to get used to 'em, you know. There's always some little cut or knock that needs seeing to. Same with football. I mean, I was here only a few weeks ago for those bruised ribs. When they tell you nothing's broken you feel better right away.'

That casual comment reminded both of them that they were here to see someone who did have broken bones and might not feel better for months, if then. Jakki had supplied them with Foggy's ward number and it wasn't hard to find in spite of a maze of long corridors and unexpected turnings.

Although this was the first time they'd been on their own together since that unforgettable evening with Andrea in the summer-house there wasn't any awkwardness between them. As if by common consent they didn't mention her at all. Instead, Danny was perfectly happy to chat about Davey's sister, Katie, a 'real flyer, I'll bet' as he described her. Kieren was content to listen to that, too, because these days he was amazed by how often he thought about Andrea: every two or three minutes, it seemed. She'd told him that Danny was history: in any case, she'd never allowed him to be the special kind of friend Kieren had so quickly become.

'Listen, Kieren, something I've got to tell you,' Danny said anxiously, putting his hand on his friend's arm. 'You know that Foggy called me about joining his team next season? Well, I didn't really give it a second thought. I'll always stick with the Kings.'

'Me, too,' Kieren agreed.

'Doesn't mean I won't try to get the captaincy back off you one day, though,' Danny grinned.

Their smiles were instantly wiped away by the sight of Foggy, one leg hoisted quite high in the air by a pulley-with-weights arrangement, his head and left arm bandaged, his face as white as the sheets covering the rest of him. His bed was at the far end of the ward and Kieren tried to avoid looking at any of the other occupants. A TV set was on and a couple of men in dressing-gowns were watching a chat show.

'Hey, Foggy, great to see you,' Kieren greeted him as cheerfully as he could manage. 'How're you feeling?'

'Lousy,' replied Foggy, opening both eyes. He appeared genuinely surprised to see them. 'Can't move a muscle – well, hardly one.'

Danny couldn't take his eyes off the leg that had been lifted to an angle of about 45 degrees. It was the weirdest sight. 'Why's your leg up in the air like that, Fogs?'

'Because it's broken, you clown, why d'you think? Supposed to help the bits of bone knit together in the right places. Or something like that. Feels awful, I tell you. Got pins stuck in it as well. Holding things together.'

Abashed, Danny apologized. Kieren took the opportunity to hand over a bundle of soccer magazines. 'Most of them are from Dominic, he gets 'em regularly,' he explained. 'He wanted you to have them to help pass the time until . . . until . . .'

'Can't hold 'em properly,' Foggy pointed out, gesturing towards his bandaged arm. 'I told his mum not to send them when she mentioned it. I also told her Dom was going to join the Giants, like you two.'

That startled his visitors more than anything else they'd seen or heard so far. 'Is that true, Fogs?' Danny asked. 'He's never said anything like that to us, has he, KK?'

Keiren shook his head. There was a pause before Foggy answered and they watched him bite his lip, perhaps because of his pain. 'No, I don't think he'd've come over to us.

But I wanted to get back at Jane Allenby for getting rid of me. I've never forgiven her, never will. I also told her you two were joining the Giants as well.'

Kieren and Danny exchanged glances. 'But we weren't, were we, Dan?' Kieren ventured.

'Definitely not,' Danny confirmed.

'Yeah, but she's bound to wonder in the future,' Foggy said. 'She won't be sure if you're loyal to the Kings any more, will she?'

'That's a bit rotten, Foggy,' Kieren told him in a mild tone. He thought it was much worse than that but he sensed he shouldn't risk saying something that might further damage Foggy's precarious health.

'Maybe, but I told you I wanted to get my own back on Ma Allenby,' Foggy went on. 'Anyway, you might all change your minds soon. The Kings are rubbish – you were just dead lucky to get a draw on Sunday. You'll need a good team to play for next season. My Giants.'

Neither of his listeners felt any need to defend the Kings; they knew the Kings had recovered brilliantly against Scorton and probably had been unlucky not to win.

'Do you think you will be leading the Giants next season, Foggy?' Kieren asked cautiously to change the subject.

To their surprise Foggy turned his face away and for several moments there was just silence apart from the sound of the TV. Anxiously Kieren and Danny looked at each other, fearful that they'd caused their old team-mate real pain. Kieren was just about to say something, anything, when Foggy spoke in a low but clear voice.

'Don't know,' he told them mournfully. 'Nobody'll tell me anything. But I hear 'em whispering round my bed. Look, I need the nurse. Just tell her, will you? I don't think you'd better stay any longer.' There was a pause before he said: 'Thanks for coming.'

Hastily they stood up, eager to get help for him. His face was still turned away and so they couldn't see his expression. 'Cheers, Fogs. See you soon,' Danny said softly. 'Bye,' Kieren echoed.

A nurse was returning to the ward as they reached the entrance. Danny told her that Marc had asked for her but he felt compelled to add: 'Is he going to be all right? I mean, will he be able to play football again?'

The nurse's lips tightened before she replied. Then she asked: 'Do you all play for the same team?'

'Not exactly, but he's a good mate of ours,' Kieren told her.

'Well, it's just too early to say, but it is a very bad injury,' she replied. 'Now I'd better see what he wants. I'm sure your visit will have done him some good, boys. Bye.'

They didn't speak again until they were clear of the hospital buildings, both deep in their own thoughts about what they'd seen and how they felt about it. They hadn't intended to stay long, anyway, because Jakki Kelly had warned them that Foggy wasn't finding it easy to relate to visitors. But all the ones so far had been adults, so no one knew how he would relate to those of his own age.

'Never to play football again,' Danny murmured at last. 'Can you imagine it, Kier?'

Kieren shook his head. He knew his eyes must be full of tears and he'd never felt quite like this before. 'D'you know what surprised me?' he said, but didn't wait for an answer. 'His voice. Sometimes I could hardly hear him. That's the total opposite of the real Foggy, isn't it? You know, the old booming Foghorn.

'Tell you something else,' he continued, now that his eyes were clearer and he could think straight. 'When I saw him about the Giants he wanted me to call him Marc. Said he'd got rid of being Foggy. Didn't even like it. But he didn't say anything about that today, did he?'

'Not a word. Just clinging to the past with us, I suppose.'

'That's all he's got left to cling to,' Kieren remarked. 'Seems a bit rotten to say this now, Dan, but I'm so glad I never *really* thought of joining the Giants. The Kings mean everything to me, you know.'

'To me, too,' his team-mate agreed.

As half-time approached at Yorkhill Jane Allenby had the impression that the Kings were easing up. In a way, that was surprising because they were leading 2–0 and looking in complete control of the game. But then, just about everything had been in their favour so far. Yorkhill really lived up to their name and the Kings, winning the toss, had chosen to play down the slope. What's more, there was a strong wind blowing at their backs. Normally the home team, a middle-of-the-table side, liked to play downhill first in order to try and establish an advantage at the interval.

This time they hadn't got what they wanted and their coach seemed to be berating them just for losing the toss. He could hardly complain about their work-rate or the skills they were displaying. Their luck, though, was out.

The Kings' first goal was a fluke. Oats, charging down the right flank with the ball at his feet, had responded to Davey's raised arm. The striker was out on the left, unmarked at that moment. As ever, he was confident he'd score if only he got a decent pass. Oats tried his best but he over-hit it and, at the same time, imparted some spin. The ball flew high, was caught by a fierce gust and carried over the goalkeeper's head before it dipped into the net. It looked like a spectacular, long-distance volley and Oats celebrated as if it were the goal of a lifetime. As his coach and most of his team-mates recognized, it was sheer luck.

Yorkhill Eagles, to their credit, weren't unnerved by that setback. With renewed endeavour and some intelligent passing they set off in search of an equalizer. Harry Greenland's height and athleticism denied them on two occasions before they broke through on goal. The rest of the time the Kings' well-marshalled defence relieved them of the ball or pushed it away to safety. Kieren was in particularly fine form and so, she was glad to see, was Dominic. The hesitancy he'd been guilty of from time to time had gone. Today he was quick and decisive. Jane had said nothing to him about Marc's allegations because she simply didn't believe them. She was equally sure about Kieren's and Danny's loyalty to the Kings. None of them would want to abandon a team that had won a Championship and, they'd promised her, would do so again.

Reuben, given a lot of freedom in midfield, set up the second goal. Up to that point he'd tended to lay the ball off with his first touch, usually finding either Josh or Davey with ease. This time he made use of the space ahead of him. Receiving a pass from Kieren, he took the ball at pace past two opponents before swerving out to the left just when it seemed he must arrow-in on goal. On the other flank Josh was calling for the ball, a ploy which attracted the attention of two Eagles defenders.

But it was Davey, accelerating in startling fashion, who homed in on a scissors movement, took the ball in his stride and fired a low unstoppable shot into the net before the keeper could even begin a dive.

'Oh YES!' Jane exulted. Cleverly crafted by Lefty, the goal was scored with all of Davey's deadly efficiency and accuracy. It was the moment she sensed the nightmare start to the Kings' post-Championship season was really over.

'Oh yes, indeed!' enthused Jakki Kelly, standing beside her. 'That was just beautifully done, wasn't it?' It occurred to Jane that earlier in the season Jakki would surely have mentioned that Kieren contributed the first significant pass that led to Davey's goal.

At half-time the coach felt she needed to do little more than encourage her team to go on playing in the same way in the second half. A couple of matches ago she'd feared she was being too soft with them, allowing them to suggest how and where they should operate. Yet it was clear now that they were dovetailing splendidly. Josh was revelling in his role as striker and proving to be an ideal partner for Davey, while the defence was looking as solid as last season's. Kieren's captaincy was impressive: he was vocal when necessary, tactful and invariably calm.

Jakki had confided how much he'd been affected by the visit to Foggy in hospital. 'When he returned he didn't say much. But there was one remark I won't forget: "Mum, I'm going to get as much as I can out of playing for the Kings so that I'll always remember the good days." Tells you a lot, that, doesn't it, Jane?'

So far as the coach could tell, Danny was much the same as usual in spite of his losses. 'Although I must say, Jakki, that he is very helpful to me, always wanting to do whatever he can for anyone. He shows no resentment at all at being replaced by Harry.' She sensed, though, that it was diplomatic not to say anything about Danny's loss of the captaincy to Kieren's mum.

Even though he'd been chatting to Katie Stroud for much of the first half, Danny had made a point of joining in the half-time team discussions. He'd even joked with Andrea who, as Jane had been surprised to note, cheered Kieren every time he had the ball. Was Kieren's friendship with her one of the reasons he was playing so well? Jane had no way of knowing that, but she hoped so. Certainly it was obvious that Katie was having a good effect on Danny.

The wind hadn't abated much by the start of the second half and so the Kings knew it was going to be a slog for the rest of the match. It became more than that when the Eagles cut the deficit within five minutes. This time, the luck was with them, although in Jane's view it wasn't that so much as rank bad refereeing.

Inevitably, the Eagles had swooped down the hill to attack in force from the outset. Rodale were holding them comfortably enough until a red-and-white-shirted striker gained possession on the edge of the box, weaved his way inside and then fell flat on his face when challenged for the ball by Dominic. Without a moment's hesitation the ref blew for a foul and pointed dramatically at the spot. Dominic and Harry were advancing angrily on the official when Kieren grabbed their arms and pulled them away.

'A blatant dive, that's what it was!' Jakki complained bitterly. 'Everybody else in the ground must know that. Except that, that stupid ref!'

Jane just nodded. She was thinking about how Harry Greenland might cope with the kick. At least he seemed to have calmed down since Kieren spoke to him. But it could have a crucial effect on the game, coming so early in the second half and with the Eagles having the slope and the gale on their side.

It was Yorkhill's skipper, a strongly built central defender, who ran up to strike the ball with his left foot. Harry, who'd been jigging up and down on his line to put the kicker off, didn't dive too soon. He waited until foot met ball. So he flung himself in the right direction. Had his arm been a few centimetres longer he probably would have reached the ball.

Instead, it flicked past his finger-tips into the back of the net. Yorkhill Eagles 1, Rodale Goal Kings 2.

'Tough luck, Harry! Good try, though,' Jane sang out to him. 'Yeah, good effort,' Danny agreed as he and Katie stood beside her.

The Eagles must have felt that their turn had come to get goals by pouring players down their favourite slope. The Kings, however, were resolute in their defensive strategies and Jane had few worrying moments. In their own way, they were playing with just as much gusto as the Eagles. So, as the minutes started to run out, it was Yorkhill who first began to fade, frustrated by their failure to get the goal they needed for at least a point. Then, three minutes from the final whistle, they knew they were going to get nothing out of the game as the Kings scored again.

Just when Jane was thinking about giving him a rest by putting on a sub, Davey, who'd had an outstanding game and zestfully supported the midfield when they were under pressure started a darting run across the Eagles' back line. Until, that is, he was brought down on the very edge of the box. Although Davey emerged unscathed it was a bad enough foul for the offender to be shown the yellow card.

Reuben lined up the kick, there was a flurry of movement in the penalty area as various players made decoy runs, and then he brilliantly curled the ball over the badly made wall and into the net off the far upright. The acclaim from the away supporters that greeted the goal couldn't have been more enthusiastic if Reuben had won a cup final for them. Instead, it was just the Kings' first victory of the season.

Jane was overjoyed. 'That's it!' she cried. 'We're back. I don't know how long it's going to take to reach the top again, but we will.'

Jakki was beaming, too. She hugged Jane and then told her: 'Well, now you can put your "Best Coach" sweatshirt on again, can't you?'

'Oh, I will, definitely. But not until we *are* on top again. Don't know exactly when that will be, but I just *know* it will happen.'

Then, as the ref put his whistle to his lips

for the last time in this game, Jane dashed on to the pitch to embrace her revitalized team.